CW00495741

The MYSTERIES of MERLIN

About the Author

One of the most respected writers and teachers in the occult field today, John Michael Greer has written more than fifty books on esoteric traditions, nature spirituality, and the future of industrial society. An initiate in Druidic, Hermetic, and Masonic lineages, he served for twelve years as Grand Archdruid of the Ancient Order of Druids in America (AODA). He lives in Rhode Island with his wife Sara. He can be found online at www.EcoSophia .net.

CEREMONIAL MAGIC
FOR THE DRUID PATH

The MYSTERIES of
MERLIN

JOHN MICHAEL GREER

LLEWELLYN PUBLICATIONS
WOODBURY, MINNESOTA

FIRST EDITION
First Printing, 2020

Cover design by Shannon McKuhen
Editing by Nicole Borneman
Interior art on pages 74, 95, 96, 97 by Eugene Smith. All other art by the Llewellyn Art
    Department

Llewellyn Publications is a registered trademark of Llewellyn Worldwide Ltd.

Library of Congress Cataloging-in-Publication Data (Pending)
ISBN: 978-0-7387-5949-4

Llewellyn Publications
A Division of Llewellyn Worldwide Ltd.
2143 Wooddale Drive
Woodbury, MN 55125-2989
www.llewellyn.com

Printed in the United States of America

Other Books by John Michael Greer

Atlantis

The Celtic Golden Dawn

Circles of Power

The Coelbren Alphabet

Earth Divination: Earth Magic

Elementary Treatise of Occult Science

Encyclopedia of Natural Magic

The Golden Dawn

Inside a Magical Lodge

Monsters

Natural Magic

The New Encyclopedia of the Occult

Paths of Wisdom

The Secret of the Temple

Secrets of the Lost Symbol

The UFO Phenomenon

Contents

Introduction

This book sets out a system of self-initiation that is based on ancient Celtic Pagan spirituality but uses the tools of modern ceremonial magic. That combination, though it has roots going back many centuries, may startle readers familiar with the attitudes of today's Pagan and occult communities, so a few words of explanation are probably necessary here.

For many decades now, an awkward fissure has run through the middle of the magical scene in most English-speaking countries. On one side are ceremonial magicians, who practice complex magical disciplines based mostly on the Hermetic tradition of ancient times as reworked in the Renaissance and then again in the modern magical revival. On the other side are Pagans, Heathens, and others who practice a range of religious, spiritual, and magical practices founded on ancient polytheist faiths. Druidry, my own spiritual home, has long been poised even more awkwardly between the two sides of the fissure, embracing elements of both movements and regarded with a certain amount of suspicion by the more doctrinaire members of both camps.

Less than a century ago, however, that split did not yet exist. It's a matter of historical record, for example, that Dion Fortune—one of the twentieth century's most influential occultists—was also among the pioneers of what became the Neopagan movement and celebrated public rituals in honor of Pan and Isis in London in the late 1930s.[1] Many other occultists of her time

---

1. For details of these rites, see Knight, *Dion Fortune's Rites of Isis and Pan*, 2013.

occupied the same comfortable middle ground between Pagan spirituality and ceremonial magic without seeing any contradiction between the two.

In the second quarter of the twentieth century, a number of Druid groups in Britain set out to take that fusion of occultism and Paganism a major step further by reworking the Golden Dawn tradition of ceremonial magic so that it used Druid symbolism and called on the powers of Pagan Celtic deities. For complex historical reasons, those traditions faded out after the Second World War, but scraps of their teachings survived. As a Druid and a Golden Dawn initiate, I found those scraps tantalizing and eventually set out to reverse engineer a complete system of Druid ceremonial magic along the same lines set out by those pioneering Druid mages of the 1920s and 1930s. The system that resulted saw print in 2013 with the publication of my book *The Celtic Golden Dawn*.

That book got an enthusiastic welcome from Druids and others who wanted to practice ceremonial magic but weren't comfortable with the way that existing traditions relied on names and symbols drawn from Judeo-Christian sources. Several similar projects are currently underway to provide effective techniques of ceremonial magic to Pagans, Heathens, polytheists, and others who are drawn to ceremonial magic but want to invoke their own gods and goddesses in magical rites.

At the same time, the toolkit of ceremonial magic has unexpected gifts to offer today's rebirth of the old polytheist faiths. Dion Fortune's rites of Isis and Pan, mentioned above, point to one of these. Using methods derived from her background in Golden Dawn ceremonial magic, Fortune crafted rituals that filled the same role, and invoked some of the same powers, as the mystery initiations of the classical Pagan world. Her rites are worth careful study and, for those drawn to them, ritual reenactment. At the same time, they point toward possibilities that have not been explored in the Western world in sixteen centuries.

As the first chapter of this book shows, the ancient mysteries—this is the traditional name for rituals of initiation linked to seasonal cycles and based on the mythic narratives of Pagan gods and goddesses—played an important role in the spiritual lives of people in the classical world. Those rituals were lost many centuries ago and in all probability will never be recovered.

As Dion Fortune showed, however, it is entirely possible to use the methods of ceremonial magic to create new rituals that will serve the same purpose.

Fortune's rituals were designed to be performed by a group of ritualists for an audience, the way that some of the ancient mysteries seem to have been done. There is another option, however, and that is the way of self-initiation. Ceremonial magicians have known for centuries that the same effects produced by a formal initiation in a temple or lodge, conferred by a team of experienced ritualists on a candidate, can also be produced by an individual aspirant in solitude by the repeated practice of an appropriately designed set of ceremonies and meditations.

That was the method I used in *The Celtic Golden Dawn*, so that students of the system could initiate themselves into it by their own perseverance and hard work. The same principle can be used to self-initiate into an equivalent of the ancient mysteries, and that is the option I have set out to provide here. The mystery I chose for this working, though poorly documented, also has much of value in its own right to teach today's spiritual seekers: the rites once practiced in honor of an archaic Celtic god whose myths come down to us in garbled and fragmentary form as the legends of Merlin.

The process of researching, developing, and writing this book has led me in directions I wasn't expecting when I started out. I had no idea in the beginning that I would uncover crucial clues to the origins of Freemasonry or that the legends I followed would point back to a system of spiritual transformation after death that was already ancient when Stonehenge was new. Still, such things happen when you research magical traditions. I hope my readers will find the adventure as fascinating as I did.

Several acknowledgments are appropriate here. Special thanks are owed first of all to R. J. Stewart, whose books on the Merlin tradition introduced me to the archaic figure behind the pop culture icon of Merlin, who offered me much-needed words of encouragement at a difficult point in my career many years ago, and who generously gave me several helpful books on the system of magic he teaches and practices. My understanding of the Merlin legends have also been shaped by conversations with Richard Brzustowicz Jr., Philip Carr-Gomm, and David Spangler.

In carrying out the research for this book, I had the help of the librarians and collections of the South Cumberland branch of the Allegany County

Public Library System, Cumberland, MD; the Lewis J. Ort Library at Frostburg State University, Frostburg, MD; the Weaver branch of the East Providence Public Library System, East Providence, RI; and the library of the Grand Lodge of the Ancient and Honorable Society of Free and Accepted Masons of the State of Rhode Island and Providence Plantations, East Providence, RI. My thanks go to all.

CHAPTER ONE
Rites of Initiation

Initiation is one of the central themes of the inner traditions of Western spirituality. The word "initiation" itself comes from the Latin term *initiatio*, which means "beginning," and this is what initiation is: the beginning of a spiritual path, or of a definite stage within that path; the dawn of a new relationship with the inner powers that guide human life and the human spirit.

There are many different forms of initiation, many ways to embark on the adventure of the spirit that initiation sets in motion. This book explores one of them. While the way of initiation presented here has its roots in ancient traditions that were once enacted by thousands of people in elaborate temples, the mystery initiations of Merlin's Wheel have been designed so that you can practice them by yourself in the privacy of any convenient room or outdoor space, using relatively simple and inexpensive material and supplies, and rituals that anyone can perform. All it requires is a willingness to learn a set of eight ceremonies and practice them at regular intervals around the cycle of the year.

In every way of initiation, preparation is important. As you begin learning about the way of Merlin's Wheel, it's important to have a clear idea of what the ceremonies are supposed to do, and that in turn is best grasped by understanding the historical roots of the system you'll be practicing. To do that, we need to make a leap of imagination across twenty-five centuries to witness one of the classic forms of initiation in the Western world: the ancient mysteries.[2] The initiations of Merlin's Wheel are modeled on those archaic initiation ceremonies and rely on the same basic principles. Knowing something about the ancient mysteries and their traditions will help you understand the work ahead.

†HE Ancient Mysteries

The month of Boedromion, roughly the same as our September, was a special time in the city of Athens in classical times. On the fourteenth of that month, heralds from the little town of Eleusis, some twenty miles away from Athens, brought certain sacred and secret things concealed in lidded baskets and placed them for safekeeping in a temple in the city.[3] The next day, everyone who intended to take part in the sacred events to follow gathered in the Agora, the central market place of Athens, to pay the initiation fee (15 drachmas, about ten days' wages for an ordinary worker), register with the officials who supervised the ceremonies, and hear the formal proclamation of the mysteries. Participation in the mysteries was not limited to any one gender, ethnicity, or social class; men and women from every corner of Greece and the surrounding countries and from every walk of life assembled to take part in the rites.

On the sixteenth, the ceremonies themselves began. All the participants rode in carts and wagons, the ordinary transport of the time, for the eight-mile trip from Athens to the seashore. (The modern equivalent would be taking a chartered bus.) There they purified themselves by bathing in salt water and offering sacrifices to Demeter and Persephone, the goddesses of the Eleusinian mysteries. The seventeenth was devoted to sacrifices in Athens' great temples. On the eighteenth, the streets of Athens were all but deserted as those who had purified themselves stayed indoors, fasting, to get ready for the events of the following day and night.

On the nineteenth, still fasting, all the participants left Athens on foot, walking in a long procession toward Eleusis, following a road called the Sacred Way. The heralds from Eleusis and a group of priestesses, carrying the

---

2. The word "mystery" (from the Greek *mysterion*) meant "ritual of initiation" originally, and only got its meaning of "something unknown" centuries later. Scholars still use the term "the ancient mysteries" to refer to the set of archaic initiation rituals discussed here.

3. To this day, nobody knows what they were.

sacred things in their baskets, led the procession. Behind them came the others, those who were attending for the first time, who were called *mystai* or "initiates," and those who had witnessed the rite before, who were called *epoptai* or "viewers." All the participants joined in the sacred chant *Iacch' o Iacche*, invoking Iacchos the fertility spirit, and waved green branches in rhythm with the words. At one place along the route, the wayfarers drank cups of a sacred beverage called *kykeon*, made of barley water flavored with herbs. At another, masked figures shouted mockery at them and made obscene gestures.

After sunset, as the stars came out overhead, the procession reached Eleusis, filed through the streets of the town by torchlight, passed through a ceremonial gateway into the sacred precincts, and walked along the traditional path past the mouth of a cave. At the end of the path was a vast temple, the Telesterion. Into it the heralds and priestesses led the way, and the others followed. There they were met by the Hierophant, the chief priest of Eleusis, and experienced the secret initiation ritual of the Eleusinian mysteries.[4]

What happened in that ritual? No one knows. We know that the traditions of Eleusis centered on the myth of the goddess Persephone's abduction by Hades, the god of the underworld, and her mother Demeter's search for her. According to the traditional tale, when the wandering Demeter came to Eleusis in her search disguised as a poor old woman, the people of the town welcomed her hospitably and offered her comfort in her grief. In her gratitude, after Persephone was restored to her, Demeter gave the townsfolk two mighty gifts. The first was the art of agriculture—the ancient Athenians believed that it was at Eleusis that the very first fields were sown with barley—and the second was a ceremony that would admit human beings into the presence of the gods and goddesses, and ensure them a hospitable welcome in the underworld when they died. That ceremony, the ritual of the Eleusinian mysteries, was at first enacted on a simple threshing floor, then in a small temple, and thereafter in a series of larger temples, culminating in the vast Telesterion of classical times.

Famous as the Eleusinian mysteries were, they were anything but unique. All over the ancient world, mystery initiations of various kinds were performed

---

4. I have based this account largely on Burkert, *Greek Religion*, 285–90, and Parke, *Festivals of the Athenians*, 55–72.

by people of all ranks of society. Most towns in Greece and the Greek-speaking countries surrounding it had their own mysteries. These were celebrated each year at a point in the seasonal cycle defined by tradition, though not all of them had anything obvious to do with the seasonal cycle. Some of them, such as the mysteries of the Cabeiri at Samothrace and the mysteries of Artemis at Ephesus, were nearly as famous as the mysteries of Eleusis; others were purely local affairs. Each of them centered on a traditional story about the gods, which was enacted in the ritual of initiation.

Famous or otherwise, all the ancient mysteries started out rooted in specific places. Until late in classical times, Eleusis was the only place you could receive the initiations of the Eleusinian mysteries. If you wanted to be initiated into the Andanian mysteries, similarly, you had to travel to the Greek city of Messene at the right season of the year, and either bring a tent or rent one once you got there; this particular set of mysteries was celebrated in a grove of cypress trees by the ruins of the old city of Andania, not far from Messene, and everyone taking part in the mystery initiation camped out in the grove for the duration of the rites.[5]

The flip side of this focus on specific places was a remarkable tolerance for difference between one mystery tradition and another, even among those who revered the same deities. The Andanian mysteries just mentioned also focused on the story of Demeter and Persephone, but nobody ever seems to have tried to start a fight between Andania and Eleusis over who had the "right" ceremonies! In fact, a third set of mysteries of Demeter and Persephone, with a different set of ceremonies, was celebrated every spring at the town of Agrai, not far from Athens, and it became customary for people to be initiated at Agrai first, wait a year, then receive the initiation at Eleusis.

In the same way, different ways of celebrating the mysteries of the same deities became common all over the ancient world. The details varied but the principle was always the same: by participating in the reenactment of a sacred story at a certain point in the seasonal cycle, the initiates of the mysteries established an inner connection with the spiritual realities that lay behind that story. That same principle underlies the rituals presented in this book.

---

5. Meyer, *The Ancient Mysteries*, 49–59. Descriptions of the event make it sound rather like some modern outdoor Pagan festivals.

†HE EVOLUTION OF †HE ΠYSTERỊES

The habit of keeping the mysteries local didn't remain in place forever. Early on in Greek history, one mystery initiation—the Dionysiac mysteries, centered on the myth of the birth and triumph of the god Dionysos—broke free of its original location in Thrace, north of Greece proper, and began to be celebrated all over the ancient world. Once the Roman Empire was established, and roads and maritime trade routes made travel easy from one end of the ancient world to another, many other traditional mysteries started to spread in the same way.

New mystery rituals were also created in the Roman era, and nearly all of these took to the roads immediately. Among the most popular of these new initiations were the mysteries of Mithras, the Persian god of light. The Mithraic mysteries, unlike most other mysteries, admitted only men, and there were seven degrees of Mithraic initiation, rather than a single ritual in which all participated. The candidate for initiation in the rites of Mithras began by receiving the degree of Corax (Raven), and ascended thereafter, after passing tests of his courage and loyalty, through the further degrees of Nymphus (Bridegroom), Miles (Soldier), Leo (Lion), Perses (Persian), Heliodromus (Runner of the Sun), and Pater (Father).[6]

The mysteries of Mithras became extremely popular among Roman legionary soldiers, sailors, and government officials. Like Freemasonry in Britain and America during the nineteenth century, the Mithraic mysteries became a bond of community among men from many different backgrounds. Wherever you went in the Roman world, if you were an initiate of Mithras, you could count on a welcoming community and help in times of trouble. It's a measure of the popularity of these mysteries that Mithraea—the distinctive underground temples where these mysteries were celebrated—have been found by archaeologists in every part of the world where the Roman Empire had a presence.

Another very successful new mystery cult centered on the story of the Egyptian goddess Isis, her search for the body of her murdered husband Osiris, Osiris's resurrection from the dead, and the conception and birth of their son Horus. The Isiac mysteries, as they were called, were originally invented and

---

6. Meyer, *The Ancient Mysteries*, 200.

celebrated by Greek settlers in Egypt after the conquests of Alexander the Great and spread rapidly across the ancient world once the Romans made travel easy and safe. The mystery temples of Isis, like those of Mithras, can be found in every corner of the Roman world. The mysteries of Isis were so popular that their most distinctive visual image—the goddess Isis with her son Horus in her lap—was plagiarized by Christianity later on to create the familiar image of the Virgin Mary and the infant Christ.

The mysteries of Attis and the Great Mother, finally, were originally celebrated in what is now Syria and Lebanon, but spread to Greece early on, and later found their way all over the ancient world. These mysteries had to do with the myth of Attis, the son of the Great Mother, yet another of the many ancient gods who died and rose again. While its rites were open to both men and women, the mysteries of the Great Mother came to be primarily women's mysteries, and it was fairly common in late Roman times for a Mithraeum and a temple of the Great Mother to be established at the same time in the same community, so that men and women each had their own initiations and rituals to celebrate.[7]

As with the Eleusinian mysteries, the rites performed in these initiations still remain a complete mystery—in several senses of the word! The initiates of every mystery cult pledged themselves to strict secrecy. Then as now, there were always people who failed to take their oaths seriously, but once Christianity seized political power across the Roman world, written accounts of mystery rituals seem to have been systematically destroyed.

This even extended to accounts by Christian writers. In the first two books of his encyclopedic *Refutation of All Heresies*, for example, the Christian bishop Hippolytus claimed to have revealed all the secrets of the Egyptian and Chaldean mysteries—that is, the mysteries of Isis and of Attis and the Great Mother. While the rest of his book survives, those two chapters were destroyed long ago, and so was the summary of their contents at the beginning of the tenth book of Hippolytus' work. Modern scholars have pointed out that this was almost certainly a deliberate act of censorship.[8]

---

7. Weston, *From Ritual to Romance*, 164–70.

8. Ibid., 152.

Only a few very carefully veiled accounts of mystery rituals survive. The philosopher Sallust, for example, who discusses the mysteries of the Great Mother in his book *On the Gods and the World*, tells us that the celebration of those mysteries begin with a period of partial fasting in which the initiates abstain from grains and certain other foods Sallust doesn't name. Next comes the cutting of a pine tree, and a period of mourning and total fasting. Next, the fast is broken by drinking milk, and there follows a period of festivity, when the initiates wear crowns and celebrate the risen Attis.[9]

Another account of a mystery ritual, the most detailed that survives, is found in the *Picatrix*, an Arabic manual of occultism compiled by an anonymous author in the tenth century out of many older books. One of the many rituals included in the *Picatrix* is an initiation ritual practiced in late Pagan times in the Greek-speaking countries of the ancient Middle East. Like the mysteries of Mithras, it was a male mystery, and it was conferred on boys when the Sun was in the sign Scorpio, between October 23 and November 21 each year. Each candidate would be dressed in red garments and would stand in front of a brazier while the initiators recited sacred words and burned tamarisk seeds on the hot coals. The tamarisk seeds burst and went flying across the room, and the boy had to keep facing the brazier the whole time— if he turned away, so that any of the burning seeds left burn marks on the back of his garments, he was disqualified from continuing with the initiation.

Once he passed this test of courage, the candidate was taken to another place and blindfolded. There, beneath an upraised spear, he took a solemn oath of secrecy. Once he took the oath, the blindfold was removed and a rooster was sacrificed above his head so that he was bathed in its blood. He was then an initiate and could wear the emblem of the mystery he had taken part in: a ring bearing the image of an ape.[10] What gods were invoked and what myth relived in this mystery remains a puzzle for future research.

The ritual recounted in the *Picatrix* was experienced only once, by boys preparing for manhood. Most other initiations, as already mentioned, were experienced more than once, and the division between *mystai*, first-time initiates, and *epoptai*, those who witnessed the rites more than once, came to be used

---

9. Sallust, *On the Gods and the World*, 20–23.

10. Greer and Warnock, *Picatrix*, 180–81.

in many mysteries. Over the centuries that these rites were enacted, it became clear to many initiates that repeated attendance strengthened and amplified the effect of the first passage through the rituals. As philosophers reflected on the experience of attending the mysteries, they came to understand the sacred narratives at the heart of the mystery ceremonies in a new way.

From this perspective, myths are things that never happened but always *are*. They express spiritual truths too profound to be communicated in any more direct way. By enacting those myths in dramatic form, and experiencing them over and over again, participants in the mysteries attune themselves to the unseen heart of being, and grow subtly but surely in wisdom and insight as a result. From this perspective, celebrating the mysteries becomes a way of drawing closer to the divine realities of the cosmos.

In the latter years of the ancient world, as this way of understanding the mysteries spread, the mystery rites became regular seasonal events that every worshiper of the old gods and goddesses attended as a matter of course. Young men and women growing up in Pagan families could look forward to their first initiation as *mystai* as soon as they were old enough, then continued to take part in the rites the next year, and every year after that, as *epoptai*. This was the state the mysteries had reached when Christian persecution drove them underground.

†HE MYSTERIES AND †HEIR LEGACY

It's considered impolite in many circles to point this out nowadays, but Christianity started out as just another mystery cult, scarcely distinguishable from all the others then being celebrated across the Roman world. Like the mysteries of Attis and the Great Mother, and many others as well, it celebrated the life, death, and resurrection of the child of a god; like all the mysteries, it invited its initiates—those who had passed through the preliminary ritual of baptism—to participate in rituals that enacted the holy story. You can see substantial parts of those original mystery rites enacted during the week leading up to Easter in the more traditional Christian churches today: the triumphal procession on Palm Sunday, the ritual mourning on Ash Wednesday, the celebrations and shouts of "He is risen!" on Easter Sunday, and the rest of it.

For complex historical reasons, though, the mysteries of Christ appealed mostly to the poor and downtrodden of the Roman world, while most of the other mysteries attracted their members mostly from the successful and educated. The bitter class divides that split late Roman society turned that difference into a source of savage hatreds, and when ambitious politicians began to exploit Christianity for the sake of political power, they learned that Christian mobs could readily be whipped into a frenzy and used to good effect in the brutal politics of the era. By the early fourth century, the Christian minority in the Roman world was large enough that an ambitious prince of the imperial house named Constantine was able to use Christianity as a weapon against his rivals and become emperor with Christian help. Within a generation, the mysteries of Christ had morphed into the earliest version of the Christian Church, and its leaders were pushing Constantine's heirs to make all other religions and mystery cults illegal.

That campaign was not finally successful for several more centuries. Long before the last Pagans were killed, exiled, or driven into hiding, however, the temples that once housed the celebrations of the mysteries were shut down and either destroyed or turned into Christian churches. Pagan *mystai* and *epoptai* who wanted to keep celebrating the mysteries responded by reworking the rituals so they could be done in private houses. In fifth-century Athens, for example, the mysteries of the Great Mother were celebrated every spring, and the Eleusinian mysteries were celebrated every autumn, in the homes of individual Pagans. These two ceremonies were among the high points of a rich seasonal cycle of ceremonies, drawn from more than a thousand years of classical Pagan tradition.

These celebrations took place during the last golden autumn of classical Paganism, an era in which great philosophers such as Iamblichus and Proclus fused Pagan religion with Greek philosophy to create what became, in later ages, the core teachings of Western occultism.[11] Though the mysteries themselves were eventually driven underground by persecution, and occultists for many centuries had to cultivate at least a veneer of Christian orthodoxy to evade punishment for heresy, the teachings themselves survived in

---

11. The word "occultism" comes from the Latin *occultus*, which means "hidden"; occultism is the hidden wisdom, the teachings that for many centuries were passed down in secret. It has nothing to do with the word "cult."

written form and reached the Renaissance, when the rich heritage of the ancient world once again drew the attention of people dissatisfied with the narrow range of spiritual options provided by Christianity.

It was in the years of the Renaissance, as scholars turned fresh eyes on the legacy of the ancient world, that the Western occult teachings we have today began to take shape. The mages and scholars of those years drew material from every source they could find, and invented new material freely to fill the gaps in what had been passed down to them, but the thread at the center of the entire enterprise was a set of insights handed down from the same late classical Pagan thinkers just mentioned. Under the name of Neoplatonism— so called because Iamblichus, Proclus, and most of their peers used the philosophy of Plato to give themselves a language of basic concepts on which to build their own ideas—those insights became a core inspiration not only for Renaissance occultism but for the entire project of the Renaissance.

Until quite recently, though, anyone in the Western world who openly left the Christian faith faced massive pushback. Laws requiring belief in Christianity remained on the books in most Western countries into the nineteenth century, and even when they were repealed—or in the case of the United States, where they didn't exist after colonial times—immense social pressure backed up by mob violence faced those who wanted to follow some other spiritual vision. Starting back in the eighteenth century, there were a few pioneers who risked everything to live according to their conscience, but by and large it wasn't until the early twentieth century that a loose alliance of Theosophists, occultists, and followers of Asian religions broke down the barriers and made it possible for today's diverse spiritual paths to exist right out in public.

The long road back to the climate of religious tolerance that existed in Greek and Roman times isn't finished yet, but enough of that distance has been covered by this point that projects as ambitious as the revival of the ancient mysteries are potentially within reach. This book is meant as a step in that direction. Its focus, however, is not one of the well-documented mystery traditions discussed already; such projects are worth pursuing, and I have discussed how they might be carried out in an appendix to this book, but the revived mystery I introduce in this book takes a different direction: toward fragmentary evidence that suggests the existence, in Roman Britain, of a mystery tradition linked in strange and compelling ways with the legend of Merlin.

†HE MYSTERIES in BRITAIN

The island of Britain was the back of the beyond in ancient times, as far north and west as you could go from the heartlands of the Roman Empire and still be in a civilized country. Even there, after the Roman conquest of Britain in the first century CE, the mysteries found a home. Archaeologists have found the distinctive temples of the Mithraic mysteries at Roman legionary forts along Hadrian's Wall in southern Scotland and among the tribes of Wales. There was also an impressive temple for the mysteries of Isis in Londinium, on the site of today's London, and an assortment of finds indicate that the Dionysiac mysteries were celebrated in private villas scattered across Roman Britain.

Archaeologists have also revealed a wealth of Roman shrines dedicated to Celtic deities. Roman culture was by and large highly tolerant in matters of religion,[12] and Roman garrisons in every corner of the Empire routinely took to worshiping the local gods and goddesses; that's how Epona, the Celtic horse goddess, became the patron goddess of the Roman imperial cavalry, and ended up with shrines very far from the British Isles. In Britain itself, hundreds of shrines dedicated to Celtic gods and goddesses have been found from the Roman period.

The Romans had the custom of identifying other people's deities with their own, a habit they called *interpretatio Romana* ("the Roman interpretation"). Every war god, to their way of thinking, was a form of Mars, every thunder god a manifestation of Jupiter, every goddess of wisdom an expression of Minerva, and so on. Thus the Celtic warrior god Toutatis appears in a Roman British inscription as Mars Toutatis, and the great healing shrine at Aquae Sulis, the modern town of Bath, was dedicated to the Celtic goddess Sul as Sulis Minerva.

The fusion of Roman and Celtic religious traditions went far beyond the mere mingling of names, however. At the shrine at Aquae Sulis just mentioned, Roman temples and rituals shared space comfortably with the ancient

---

12. Christians were persecuted by the Roman state for several centuries, but this was not for religious reasons. The act of burning incense to the *genius* (guardian spirit) of the Emperor had the same role in the Roman world that the Pledge of Allegiance has in America today. Because they refused to perform this rite, Christians were considered politically disloyal.

Celtic reverence for sacred springs. In the same way, the god Nodens—who is remembered in Irish legend as Nuada of the Silver Hand—had an important shrine at Lydney, in Gloucestershire, where Roman ceremonies were enacted in his honor and sick people slept in a special temple, hoping to receive a healing dream from the god.

Were there local mysteries celebrated in Roman Britain that enacted the myths of native Celtic deities? The question is remarkably hard to answer for certain, one way or another. The only reason that archaeologists are sure of the presence of the Mithraic, Isaic, and Dionysian mysteries in Roman Britain is that enough written evidence from elsewhere in the Roman world makes it possible to recognize the distinctive traces of these rites. If these clues didn't exist, we would only know that Mithras, Isis, and Dionysos were worshiped in Roman Britain—we would have no way of knowing that the worship in question included mystery initiations.

Thus it's entirely possible, for example, that mysteries of Sulis Minerva were celebrated at Bath and mysteries of Nodens were practiced at Lydney. The near-total lack of written records from Roman Britain makes it impossible to know one way or the other. All that can be said for certain is that many mystery cults that were widespread in the Roman world found homes in Britain, that local mystery cults celebrating the stories of local gods existed elsewhere in the Empire, that there's no good reason to think that the religious scene in Roman Britain was in any way unique, and that local mysteries that worshiped Celtic deities therefore could well have existed there during the centuries that Rome ruled Britain.

Another scrap of evidence points to a similar conclusion. In the early twentieth century, Jessie Weston, one of the premier scholars of the Arthurian legends at that time, made a strong case that the legends of the Holy Grail derived from the rituals of a Gnostic mystery cult that came to Britain in late Roman times and survived there well into the Middle Ages, if not longer.[13] Her theory has become unfashionable among scholars in recent years, but it has never been disproved, and the arguments that Weston presented to support her theory remain forceful. If she was right, the mysteries of the Grail were celebrated from late Roman times on at a specific location in the

---

13. Weston, *From Ritual to Romance*.

English county of Northumberland, a place recalled in the Middle Ages as the "chapel perilous" of the Grail legends. For reasons we'll discuss in detail shortly, that area of northern Britain is a likely area for mystery cults to have flourished in Roman times, as well as a likely area for Pagan traditions to survive after they were stamped out elsewhere in Britain.

With all this in mind, we can turn to the tangled body of legend and lore that surrounds the figure of the prophet and wizard Merlin, and begin tracing the path back from those legends to the archaic religious secret at its heart.

──── CHAPTER TWO ────
THE MYSTERIES OF MERLIN

Merlin the enchanter has become one of the stock characters of the modern imagination, but the usual image of him that people have in their heads today—the old man with the pointed hat spangled with moons and stars, and the rest of it—is a recent invention. Trace the legends back into the past and Merlin reveals himself as a much stranger and more interesting figure.[14] It's this more authentic vision of Merlin that is central to the rituals presented in this book, and so a little time spent learning about Merlin will not be wasted.

To make sense of the archaic presence of Merlin, and thus of the powers invoked in the rituals of Merlin's Wheel, it's helpful to start with the sources of the Merlin legend that date from before he was turned into a cliché. There are three broad categories of older sources: a handful of obscure Welsh documents dating from the Dark Ages, the writings of a single bestselling author of the early Middle Ages, and the poems and stories written by a galaxy of minstrels over the couple of centuries that followed that author's time. Trying to make sense of these is a challenge because they don't present a single consistent picture.

Instead, what comes through is a jumble of fragmentary images that never quite fit into a meaningful biography, or even a consistent story. That's

---

14. I am indebted to Stewart, *The Mystic Life of Merlin*; Stewart, *The Prophetic Vision of Merlin*; and Tolstoy, *The Quest for Merlin*, for my introduction to Merlin's older forms.

all but universal for legendary figures from the Dark Ages, the five centuries of chaos that engulfed Western Europe after the fall of Rome. As we'll see, though, it has deeper roots as well.

The Old Welsh writings that have to do with Merlin—or rather Myrddin, the Welsh spelling of his name—are a medley of intriguing fragments. A few very ancient poems in Welsh, laments for heroes fallen in battle in the wars of the sixth century, were supposedly written by Merlin; a passage in another ancient Welsh poem, *Y Gododdin*, refers to "the inspiration of Merlin"; the Welsh Triads, a collection of enigmatic texts that summarize old lore in sets of three, mention him a few times;[15] and a strange passage in the White Book of Rhydderch, a medieval book of Welsh stories and poems, states that before Britain was settled by human beings, its name was *Clas Myrddin*, Merlin's Enclosure. That is all—enough to make it clear that Merlin was not simply an invention of some medieval poet, but not enough to go much further.

The bestselling medieval author was Geoffrey of Monmouth, a Welsh clergyman and writer who lived during the twelfth century. Geoffrey is the reason you've heard of somebody named King Arthur. Around the year 1136, he completed his most famous work, *The History of the Kings of Britain*, a sprawling chronicle that claims to record the history of Britain from its original settlement by refugees from the Trojan War all the way up to the beginning of the Middle Ages. At the center of the entire story is the reign of King Arthur, who united the Britons against the Saxon invaders and established a brief, glorious kingdom amid the chaos of the oncoming Dark Ages—and Merlin plays a crucial role in the rise of Arthur's kingdom. While Geoffrey was never averse to concocting details to make a better story, many modern scholars now believe that he had access to oral traditions and possibly written documents as well, and used these as raw material for his tale.

The minstrels who picked up Merlin where Geoffrey left him were entertainers rather than historians. Some of them seem to have had access to ancient traditions relating to Merlin and put material borrowed from those traditions into the stories and songs they wrote. Others simply let their imaginations run wild and turned the result into lively tales that helped create the star-spangled Merlin of the modern imagination. As we try to make sense of

---

15. See Aneirin, *Y Gododdin*.

the Merlin legends in the chapter ahead, some of the themes picked up by the minstrels will provide useful clues, but a great deal of care has to be taken in sorting out authentic traditions from medieval inventions.

Merlin the Prophet

We can begin with Geoffrey of Monmouth, who provides the nearest thing to a coherent story of Merlin that can be found in any of the old sources, and whose account of Merlin is a central source for the rituals in this book. Merlin's adventures comprise just a small portion of *The History of the Kings of Britain*, where it makes up one of the tales Geoffrey recounts from the time of troubles just before Arthur's reign. As Geoffrey tells it, King Vortigern seized the British throne from its rightful heir and imposed his tyrannical rule over the land. In order to secure his power, Vortigern hired a band of Saxon mercenaries headed by the canny warlord Hengist. Once Hengist and his people had settled in Britain, though, they brought over more Saxon warriors from the mainland and set out to take Britain for their own.

Trying to protect himself from his former allies, Vortigern ordered his servants to build a strong tower on the hill of Dinas Ffaraon in northern Wales. No matter how hard the laborers worked during the day, however, each night the stones and timbers vanished into the ground. Vortigern consulted with his entourage of wizards, and they told him that the tower would only stand if the mortar for the stones was mixed with the blood of a child who had no father.

Vortigern, Geoffrey's story continues, sent messengers across the length and breadth of his kingdom in search of such a child. When the messengers came to Carmarthen in south Wales, they heard one boy shouting at another, "How dare you dispute with me? My father is a king, and you never had a father at all!" The messengers investigated and learned that the boy at whom this accusation had been flung was named Merlin, the son of a princess of that country, and no one knew who his father was.

The princess and her son were taken straight to Vortigern's court, where she admitted that she had been made pregnant by a spirit in the shape of a young man. The young Merlin then confronted the king, who admitted that he had sent for the boy to sacrifice him. Merlin asked him to send for his wizards and demanded that they explain why the tower would not stand. When they could not, Merlin told Vortigern that there was a lake beneath the hill, and two stones under the lake, and a dragon inside each stone, and the conflict of the dragons caused the tower to tumble down each night.

Vortigern ordered the workmen to dig into the hill and they found the lake; once the water was drained away, the rocks appeared, and the dragons leapt out of them and began to fight each other. As they struggled, Vortigern asked Merlin what the combat meant, and the boy burst into tears and began to prophesy. Geoffrey devoted an entire chapter of *The History of the Kings of Britain* to Merlin's prophecies, which became as popular in the Middle Ages as the prophecies of Nostradamus are today.

Thereafter, when the rightful heir Ambrosius returned to Britain and defeated Vortigern, Merlin became his counselor and built Stonehenge for Ambrosius, bringing stones across the sea from Ireland for the purpose. When Ambrosius died, in turn, Merlin advised his brother Uther. When Uther fell in love with Ygerna, the wife of the Duke of Cornwall, it was Merlin who cast a spell on Uther to give him the appearance of Ygerna's husband, and it was in this way that Arthur was conceived.

That is very nearly Merlin's last appearance in *The History of the Kings of Britain*. Once Geoffrey's hugely successful book made Merlin famous, however, the minstrels took up the theme and filled in the gaps in Merlin's biography. According to these tales, Merlin took the child of Uther and Ygerna, the future King Arthur, shortly after his birth, and had him fostered by a noble knight, the Sir Ector of later legend. When Arthur came of age, Merlin arranged for the test of the sword in the stone that proved Arthur to be the rightful king. He then guided Arthur in his wars against the rebellious barons and helped establish the peace that followed. Finally, as a very old man, he was buried alive in an underground chamber. The version most commonly remembered today, in which he fell in love with a young woman who talked him into teaching her magic and then trapped him underground to get rid of his unwanted attentions, is only one of several attempted explanations of this odd fate. As we'll see later in this chapter, it echoes themes from extraordinarily ancient lore.

As noted earlier, some of the later authors who embroidered the story of Merlin seem to have had access to authentic Celtic traditions, while others relied on Christian theology or on their own vivid imaginations to pad out the tale. Very few of them seem to have known that Geoffrey of Monmouth had more to say about Merlin. Many years after he finished *The History of the Kings of Britain*, though, Geoffrey wrote a shorter book, *The Life of Merlin*, which places Merlin in the midst of a strangely different story.[16]

According to this second account, Merlin was a king in southern Scotland who went mad and fled into the forests of Scotland in the aftermath of a great battle. His sister Ganieda tried several times to lure him back to civilization, and her husband King Rodarcus imprisoned him, hoping to bring him to his senses, but Merlin always fled back to the woods whenever he could. In time, the great poet Taliesin came to speak with him and reminded him of the distant time when the two of them had helped take the wounded King Arthur to a magical isle across the western ocean, where the king would be healed of his wounds. Thereafter, through a series of strange events and the sudden appearance of a magical spring, Merlin was restored to his senses; his sister Ganieda, now a widow, came to live with him and built an observatory with seventy windows in which Merlin could spend his final years contemplating the heavens.

Except for the scene where Taliesin describes the last voyage of Arthur, this Scottish Merlin has no apparent connection at all with the Welsh Merlin recounted in *The History of the Kings of Britain*. The lack of connection is made even more striking by the fact that both Merlin stories seem to have some historical basis. The story of Merlin and Vortigern occurs in a very old collection of Welsh historical documents, the *Historia Brittonum*, compiled by a scribe named Nennius in the ninth century. The version that Nennius put in his collection gives the wise child the name Ambrosius rather than Merlin, but Geoffrey and several other sources reconcile this by saying that Ambrosius was one of Merlin's other names.

The story of *The Life of Merlin*, though, also connects back to actual events during the early Dark Ages. The battle after which Merlin went insane, according to old British chronicles, was the battle of Arderydd in the year 573,

---

16. See Geoffrey of Monmouth, *The Vita Merlini* [The Life of Merlin].

where the Pagan king Gwenddolau was defeated by the Christian armies of the sons of Eliffer. Gwenddolau and the battle of Arderydd are mentioned in *Afallenau* (*The Apple Trees*), one of the very early Welsh poems attributed to Merlin, and the wizard's hiding place is described in both the poems and *The Life of Merlin* as the forest of Caledon, the great woodland that covered most of southern Scotland during the Dark Ages.

Geoffrey tries to turn these two distinct figures into a single Merlin, but the chronology simply won't work. Vortigern, the king who tried to sacrifice the boy Merlin, was a historical figure, a king of Britain whose reign extended approximately from 425 to 459.[17] If Merlin was a child when Vortigern died in 459, he must have been born sometime around 450, and yet the *Life of Merlin* has him not merely alive but fighting a battle in Scotland in 573, and active for many years thereafter. No actual human being could have had such a lifespan.

·

Merlin the God

To make sense of the legends is no easy task, but Geoffrey of Monmouth made it a good deal easier than it might have been. When he assembled the fragmentary records and poems about Merlin into his two narratives, he added a great deal of incident and local color—medieval writers were expected to do that—but he included as many details from his sources as he could, and changed very little. As a result, Geoffrey gives Merlin an oddly divided life. As a child and a young man he is active in Wales and southwestern Britain in the middle years of the fifth century; as an old man he is active in southern Scotland in the last quarter of the sixth century. The obvious conclusion—a conclusion already reached by medieval scholars less than a century after Geoffrey's time—is that he mistakenly ran together accounts of two different people.

Gerald of Wales, who wrote an account of his travels through his homeland in the last decade of the twelfth century, explained the matter this way:

There were two Merlins. The one called Ambrosius, who thus had two names, prophesied when Vortigern was king. He was the son of an

---

17. Morris, *The Age of Arthur*, 512.

incubus and was discovered in Carmarthen, which means Merlin's town, for it received its name from the fact that he was found there. The second Merlin came from Scotland. He was called Caledonius, because he prophesied in the Caledonian Forest.[18]

Many modern scholars who have investigated the Merlin legend have agreed with Gerald's straightforward summary. According to this theory, we have two different Merlins contributing to the legend: a Merlin Ambrosius who lived in the fifth century, and a Merlin Caledonius who lived in the sixth. The story doesn't end here, though, for there are more Merlins to consider.

In a famous 1965 study of Stonehenge, Gerald Hawkins pointed out the shadowy presence of a third Merlin.[19] He noted that Geoffrey of Monmouth, unlike later authors, had Merlin use machinery rather than magic to haul the stones of Stonehenge by sea from Ireland to Salisbury Plain, and speculated that behind Geoffrey's story might linger some distant folk memory of the actual builder of the great stone circle.

What makes this speculation plausible is that some of the stones of Stonehenge did in fact come by sea, just as Geoffrey claimed. The great gray stones that make up the largest part of the monument are local rock, of a kind found all over Salisbury Plain, but another set of smaller stones—called "bluestones" because of their color—were brought by water from quarries in the Prescelly Mountains of southwestern Wales. Wales is not Ireland, to be sure, but from the site of Stonehenge the Prescelly range lies in the same direction as Ireland, and Geoffrey can be forgiven for getting a few of the details wrong when the moving of the bluestones happened three thousand years before he wrote.

Behind these three Merlins lies a fourth, the strangest of all. This is the one referenced in the passage from the White Book of Rhydderch mentioned earlier, which says that before the first human beings settled the island of Britain, it was known as *Clas Myrddin*, Merlin's Enclosure. This makes no sense if Merlin was the name of a prophet of the fifth century or a madman of the sixth, or even of both of them; it makes only a little more sense if Merlin, or rather some fantastically archaic equivalent of that name, was the master-builder

---

18. Gerald of Wales, *The Journey Through Wales and The Description of Wales*, 192.

19. Hawkins, *Stonehenge Decoded.*

who transported the bluestones by sea and land to Stonehenge. It was Geoffrey Ashe, in a valuable 1987 essay, who pointed out that these quandaries all make perfect sense if Merlin is a god.[20]

It was actually quite common in the Dark Ages for Christian scribes to convert the gods and goddesses of the old Pagan religions into faux-historical human characters. Thus Snorri Sturluson's *Heimskringla*, a chronicle of the Norwegian kings written around 1230, redefined the god Odin as an ancient king in Asia, and the medieval Irish *Glossary of Cormac* turned the Irish sea-god Manannan mac Lir into a famous merchant of the past, whose skill as a sailor and pilot led to his being called the god of the sea.[21] If the same thing happened in the case of Merlin, it would make instant sense of all the perplexities surrounding his legend.

It's true that the sparse and fragmentary records of Pagan Celtic religion in Britain that still survive include no reference to a god called Merlin, or to any god with a name similar enough to Merlin that time might have rounded off the name into the form we know today. This is less of an objection than it might seem, though, because records of ancient Celtic religion in Britain are incredibly sparse. Very nearly the only available sources are those Roman inscriptions that include Celtic as well as Roman names for deities. Where the Celtic name has been overlaid by a Roman one, in the usual fashion of the *interpretatio Romana*, we have precisely no way of guessing what Celtic name might have been used by the native peoples of Britain for any particular "Mercury" or "Mars."

What makes this even more confusing is that most of the "names" that appear on inscriptions are actually titles. Cernunnos, the term for the antlered god of fertility and prosperity, is the title "He of the Horns"; Sucellos, the term for the hammer-swinging thunder god, is the title "the Good Striker"; Epona, the term for the horse goddess mentioned earlier, is the title "She of the Horse." The true names of these and other Celtic deities were apparently never written down, and may only have been known to an inner circle of their Druid priests and priestesses. What's more, we have no way of know-

---

20. This article appears in Stewart, *The Book of Merlin*, 17–46.
21. Ibid., 152.

ing whether more than one title might have been used for the same deity, or whether more than one deity might have been known by the same title.

The name Merlin, in fact, seems to have started out as a title rather than a name. Geoffrey of Monmouth, along with other medieval writers, claimed that Carmarthen (in Welsh, Caerfyrddin) was named after Merlin. That seems to make grammatical sense—Caerfyrddin does look like Caer-Myrddin, "Merlin's Castle," with the M changed to F according to the rules of Welsh grammar—but more recent historical research has turned this on its head. It turns out that Carmarthen in pre-Roman times was named Moridunum, the Fortress of the Sea, and this ancient name changed over the centuries to Castrum Moridunum, to Caer Myrddin, then to Caerfyrddin and Carmarthen.

And the name Merlin or Myrddin? Linguists learned a long time ago that similar words in the same language change in parallel ways over time. If you take the same linguistic transformations that turned Castrum Moridunum into Caerfyrddin and run them in reverse on the Welsh name Myrddin, you end up with the ancient Celtic title Moridunos, "He of the Sea-Fortress." The sea-fortress mentioned in the name may well have been the island of Britain itself, over which the passage in the White Book of Rhydderch says Merlin ruled. The god's true name, the name his priests and priestesses invoked in secret, is impossible to guess today.

Was Merlin, then, purely a god, and his appearances as a Dark Age prophet and wizard only garbled mythology? That is a surprisingly difficult question to answer. The line between humanity and divinity was taken seriously in ancient times, but persons of unusual holiness and power were sometimes identified by later generations as an incarnation of the god or goddess they served. (The case of Jesus of Nazareth was far less unusual at the time than modern Christians like to pretend.) Though the fragmentary surviving data won't settle the question one way or another, it is entirely possible that in the turmoil of Dark Age Britain, two priests or initiates of the god Moridunos played important historical roles—one in southern Wales in the late fifth century, the other in southern Scotland in the late sixth century—and folk memories of their deeds became mingled with the myths of Moridunos himself in the centuries that followed. This would certainly help explain why the legends of Merlin are such a jumble!

Whether or not this is what happened, at least two shrines of the god Moridunos can be identified from the legends. In his manifestation as Merlin Ambrosius, he has close ties with the town of Carmarthen in southwestern Wales. According to one set of Welsh legends, he lived at a hill named Bryn Myrddin (Merlin's Hill) near the river Tyfi, two and a half miles from Carmarthen. Local legends speak of a cave under the hill where the wizard lived and worked his magic, and where he descended into the earth and still abides today. Other traditions place him further up the Tyfi near Llandeilo, on the grounds of Dynefor Castle, where a cave close to the river has the same reputation as the one under Bryn Myrddin.

The cult of Merlin Caledonius also has a geographical location. In his valuable book *The Quest for Merlin*, using clues from old Welsh poetry as well as a later Arthurian tale, Nikolai Tolstoy tracked down the site where the Merlin of Geoffrey's second story spent his woodland days. In the Scottish county of Dumfriesshire lies a hill called Arthuret Knoll, the site of the battle of Arderydd. North of there, at the end of a long valley, a mountain named Hart Fell rises up to dominate a broad reach of the Scottish lowlands. Though Hart Fell is bare of trees today, it was once thickly forested, and rose out of dense woodland. High on its southwestern flank, a chalybeate[22] spring rises in a narrow valley that must once have been covered in deep shadow from overhanging trees. This, Tolstoy suggests on very solid grounds, is the Well of Galabes that Geoffrey describes as Merlin's woodland refuge.

Hart Fell is relevant for another reason. It is located near one of the major strongholds of Celtic Pagan religion in the early Dark Ages, a sacred place of the Celtic god Maponos or Mabon famous enough to be recorded in a late Roman geographical text now known as the Ravenna Cosmography.[23] The *locus Maponos* ("Place of Mabon") listed in that text has been identified as the modern Scots town of Lochmaben. Not far from Lochmaben is a huge boulder, the Clochmabenstane ("Stone of Mabon's Head"), where local tradition claims Pagan rituals were enacted in ancient times.

Mabon is another archaic Celtic deity of whom very little is known. His apparent name is yet another title—Maponos in the ancient British language

---

22. That is, a healing spring with water that contains dissolved iron. The famous Chalice Well at Glastonbury is another chalybeate spring.

23. Tolstoy, *The Quest for Merlin*, 204–7.

means simply "the Son." Certain inscriptions from Roman Britain refer to him. So does *The Mabinogion*, the great collection of Welsh legends, which includes a story—"Culhwch and Olwen"—in which Mabon ap Modron (literally "Son, son of Mother") is an important character.[24] Nikolai Tolstoy, in the same book mentioned above, presents evidence that Maponos was another title of the same god we know as Moridunos or Merlin. Certainly the Welsh Merlin's role as magical child, the son of a mother but not a human father, fits this title well.

This same area of lowland Scotland just mentioned, and the northern end of England immediately to the south, had been a major center for the Roman military presence in Britain. Garrisons defending the Roman province of Britannia against the wild Pictish barbarians north of Hadrian's Wall had their forts and camps there—and where the legions went, the mysteries of Mithras and other traditional Roman religious practices inevitably followed. This was one of the historical realities Jessie Weston discussed in making her case that the mysteries of the Grail had survived in northern England from late Roman times to the present, and the same case can be made for the survival of the mysteries of Moridunos-Maponos, Merlin the Mabon, in southern Scotland.

†HE †HREEFOLD DEA†H

At this point it's necessary to point out another key difference between the Welsh Merlin Ambrosius and the Scottish Merlin Caledonius: the manner of their deaths. Merlin Ambrosius, according to Celtic traditions picked up by medieval writers, went down in the earth—into a crystal cave, as some of the old texts claim—and abides there in an otherworldly form of life. Geoffrey gives Merlin Caledonius a variant of the same fate, in the form of his withdrawal into the observatory with seventy windows. Other sources suggest a far stranger death for the Merlin of Scotland, and Geoffrey himself weaves that motif into *The Life of Merlin* in a sidelong way.

According to Geoffrey's version, after King Rodarcus imprisoned Merlin and tried to bring him back to his senses, Merlin won his freedom by revealing to the king that his queen, Merlin's sister Ganieda, had been unfaithful to

---

24. See Gantz, *The Mabinogion*.

him. Ganieda set out to discredit her brother's prophetic powers by having the same boy presented to him three times, once with long hair, once with short hair and different clothing, and once dressed as a girl, while Ganieda asked him how the child would die. Merlin prophesied the first time that the boy would die by falling from a high rock, the second that he would hang from a tree, and the third that the "girl" would drown in a river. As a result of this ruse, King Rodarcus decided that Merlin must be wrong about Ganieda's behavior. Later on, however, when the boy was grown and he was hunting, he slipped from a high rock and fell headfirst into the river in such a way that one of his feet caught in the branches of a tree, and the rest of him ended up underwater. Thus he died in all three of the ways Merlin had prophesied.

According to other versions of the same story, though, it was Merlin himself who died in three different ways. A curious legend that became part of the medieval biography of St. Kentigern, the patron saint of Glasgow, tells of a madman named Lailoken who shared most of the characteristics of the Scottish Merlin, and who prophesied on three separate occasions that he would be clubbed and stoned to death, impaled on a stake, and drowned. Not long thereafter Lailoken was beaten and stoned savagely by a group of shepherds, and as he was dying of his wounds, he fell into a river, was impaled by a wooden stake in the water, and drowned. One of the two medieval accounts of Lailoken's death quotes two lines from an old poem that make it clear who the original victim of the triple death was:

Pierced by a stake, suffering by stone and by water,
Merlin is said to have met a triple death. [25]

Behind this curious tale lies the shadow of an ancient and terrible tradition. Human sacrifice was practiced now and again by most of the peoples of the ancient world.[26] The ancient Celts, according to some Greek authors, used it as a means of capital punishment for the most detested crimes. Some

---

25. Tolstoy, *The Quest for Merlin*, 171.
26. It is easy for modern people to feel a sense of smug superiority about this, but little has changed. In our more secular age, we offer up human lives to political ideologies and economic interests, rather than to gods.

of the people the Celts sacrificed were burned, some stabbed, and some shot with arrows—again, three ways of death.

A very widespread custom in cultures that practice human sacrifice is to have the victims imitate the god or goddess to whom they are offered. Thus in Scandinavia in Heathen times, for example, when human beings were offered to Odin, they were hung from a tree and then stabbed with a spear, in imitation of the god's own self-sacrifice upon the World Tree Yggdrasil. If the threefold death of Merlin Caledonius echoes an ancient rite of sacrifice once practiced on or near Hart Fell, the victims offered up to He of the Sea-Fortress may well have been struck by three different weapons, or in some other way made to pass through a threefold death of their own. As we'll see, this tradition has a surprising modern echo—one that will allow us to draw unexpected conclusions about the later history of the cult of Moridunos.

†HE CRYSTAL CAVE

A tradition stranger and even more archaic than the threefold death, in turn, lies behind the very different fate of Merlin Ambrosius. As already noted, he was believed to have descended into a cave far beneath the earth and remains there, still alive in some sense, despite all the centuries that have passed. The ancient tradition that lies behind this tale has left echoes of itself in many other legends and lands, for Merlin is far from the only master of arcane wisdom who is said to have ended his visible life in this way.

In Japan, off the other end of the Eurasian continent, a remarkably similar story is told about the wizard-saint Kōbō-Daishi, who lived from 774 to 835 CE. The founder of the Shingon sect of Buddhism, Kōbō-Daishi can fairly accurately be described as Japan's Merlin. As a young man he traveled from Japan to China, where he was initiated into the deepest mysteries of esoteric Buddhism. When he returned to Japan in 806, he became an adviser to emperors and founded the famous Shingon monastery on Mount Kōya. Countless legends describe his arcane powers. At the end of his life, he withdrew into a grotto near the monastery on Mount Kōya, and according to tradition he is still there, deep in meditation, waiting for the arrival of Miroku, the Buddha of the future.

The legend of Christian Rosenkreutz, the legendary founder of the Rosicrucians, is practically the same story. According to the seventeenth-century

Fama Fraternitatis (*Report on the Fraternity*), the first of the original Rosicrucian manifestoes, Rosenkreutz was born in Germany in 1378, and as a very
young man set off on travels that took him across the Middle East, where he
learned all the secrets of magic. Returning to Germany, he founded the Rosicrucian fraternity. At the end of his life he was buried in a mysterious vault
with seven sides. When the vault was rediscovered 120 years later, his body
was found perfectly preserved, and in his hands was a book containing the
inner secrets of Rosicrucian occultism.

Another very famous example from pop culture echoes the same theme.
The famous horror-fantasy writer H. P. Lovecraft, like many of the other fantasy authors of his time, was well informed about occultism and borrowed
various themes from occult teaching for his fiction. Cthulhu, the tentacled
Great Old One who lies "dead yet dreaming" in the lost city of R'lyeh, is a
funhouse-mirror reflection of the concept just discussed.

What lies behind these legends and the many more like them, according
to occult tradition,[27] is an archaic magical operation by which a sufficiently
knowledgeable and strong-willed person can pass into another mode of existence at death and function for many centuries thereafter as the guardian
spirit of a family, a community, or an occult school. Legends in many lands
tell of great sages and heroes of the past who descended into stone tombs beneath the earth while still alive, and the stone-chambered mounds of northern and western Europe are routinely connected with such legends.

In Japan, where stone-chambered mounds and standing stones all but
identical to those found in Britain and Ireland dot the landscape, a version
of the traditional operation was still in use in one rural area as late as the
nineteenth century. In this process, the practitioner stopped eating ordinary
foodstuffs and subsisted on a special diet of nuts, berries, bark, and pine nee-
dles. The amount of food was then gradually reduced until, by the end of the
thousand-day process, the practitioner had eaten nothing for many days. If
everything went properly, the practitioner died while seated in meditation
on the last day of the process. He was then put in a wooden coffin and buried

---

27. These have been described in detail in a variety of traditional and recent writings; see
    especially Knight, *The Secret Tradition in Arthurian Legend*, and Stewart, "The Tomb
    of a King."

in a stone chamber for three years, at the end of which his body was dug up, and found to be naturally mummified.

Several of these mummies are still on display in Buddhist temples in the isolated valley of Senninzawa—literally "Swamp of Wizards"—in Yamagata Prefecture. According to tradition, the monks who successfully completed this terrible austerity did not actually die; instead, they passed into a state of suspended animation called *nyūjō*, and like Kōbō-Daishi, they will remain in meditation until the coming of the future Buddha Miroku.[28] Local Buddhists consider these mummified monks to be *sokushinbutsu*, "living Buddhas," and revere them as potent spiritual guardians. In the temples of Senninzawa, the mummies sit in the place usually reserved for statues of the Buddha himself.

The exact details of the procedure doubtless varied from one end of Eurasia to the other, but there is good reason to think that some process not too different from this was in use in very ancient times in the British Isles. The long barrows still found all over Britain, Ireland, and other parts of northwestern Europe were the places where this was originally practiced. In the early days of the tradition, according to occult teachings on the subject, the point of the practice was much the same as at Senninzawa: those who went into the earth in the great stone barrows merged with divine and ancestral powers and became guardian spirits, sources of wisdom, power, and protection for members of local communities, still in some sense alive and powerful—just as Merlin was said to be.

Later on, in Britain and elsewhere, the tradition was abused in various ways. Kings and nobles had themselves buried in stone-chambered mounds in the hope of cheating death, and this eventually led to such vast and useless creations as the pyramids of Egypt. When the magical process behind the tradition still worked, as it sometimes did, the results were even worse.

In his commentary on the Old English epic *Beowulf*, J. R. R. Tolkien—who was a brilliant scholar of Anglo-Saxon language and traditional lore as well as a great fantasy novelist—discussed the strange word *orcnéas*, which comes from *orc*, "hell," and *néas*, "corpses." Tolkien borrowed the traditional legends of these uncanny beings to create the "barrow-wights" in *The Lord of the Rings*, but they are discussed as real beings in Old Norse and early German

28. Blacker, *The Catalpa Bow*, 87–90.

sources, and have close equivalents in the folklore and magical teachings of many other lands. Tolkien described them as "(t)hose dreadful creatures that inhabit tombs and mounds. They are not living; they have left humanity, but they are 'undead.' With superhuman strength and malice they can strangle men and rend them." [29] Later still, when the abuses of the tradition led to its abandonment across most of Eurasia, it survived in an even more corrupt and predatory form in a few regions of the world, where it contributed to the legends of vampirism.[30]

The legends of Merlin hearken back to an age long before the tradition became corrupt, when dim folk memories still recalled ancient sages who went into the earth to become one with He of the Sea-Fortress, the guardian deity of Britain itself. Since those legends cluster around Carmarthen, just as the legends of the threefold death cluster around Hart Fell, we can surmise that the legends of the god Moridunos current in southern Wales included the descent into the earth as their final element, while the legends from southern Scotland referenced the threefold death and the human sacrifices of ancient times.

Were there mystery cults connected with the god Moridunos? One crucial piece of evidence argues that there were. Despite all the centuries that separate the modern world from the days of ancient Rome, the central mythological pattern of the cult at Hart Fell, the threefold death, still survives in garbled, fragmentary, and misunderstood form in one of the few echoes of the ancient mysteries to survive into the present: the Master Mason degree of Freemasonry.

†ʜᴇ Wɪᴅᴏᴡ's Sᴏɴ

For quite a long time now, it has been fashionable in Pagan and magical circles to claim that this or that spiritual tradition has survived in secret for many centuries without changing in any way that matters. Attractive though this notion is, history shows otherwise, and a clear sense of what actually happens to spiritual traditions that are forced underground is essential to make sense of what follows. Some examples will help make this clear.

---

29. Tolkien, *Beowulf*, 165–66.

30. My book *Monsters* discusses the latter stages of this tradition; see Greer, *Monsters*, 34–51.

In 1492, to cite one of the most famous instances, King Ferdinand of Spain ordered all Jews expelled from his kingdom. Some stayed behind and pretended to be Christians, hoping that the trouble would blow over in a few years. It didn't, and for centuries thereafter their descendants had to hide from the Spanish Inquisition. In recent years, historians and folklorists in Spain and the Spanish-speaking countries of the Americas have discovered surviving families of Marranos, as these covert Jews are called. How much survives in such families of the traditions of Judaism? In most cases, only a few customs and some garbled remnants of Jewish religious lore, heavily overlaid with ideas borrowed from the Catholicism of the surrounding culture.

On the other end of Eurasia in the sixteenth century, as Japan's era of civil wars wound to an end, many Japanese on the southern island of Kyushu welcomed Jesuit missionaries and converted to Christianity. Once peace was restored by the Tokugawa shoguns, though, the Christian population was considered a massive security risk; missionaries were expelled, churches destroyed, and Japanese Christians ordered to renounce their faith on pain of death. Some of the converts continued to practice Christianity in secret. When religious freedom became law in Japan after 1945, these *Kirishitan* surfaced again. How much Catholic Christianity did they still practice? Again, a few customs and some garbled traditions survived, heavily overlaid with ideas borrowed from the Shinto and Buddhism of the surrounding culture.

Still another example has been discussed at length by William Sullivan in his fascinating book *The Secret of the Incas: Myth, Astronomy, and the War Against Time*.[31] In his research into the surviving traditions of the Inca peoples of South America's mountains, he found time and again that fragmentary elements of their lore had been preserved under a superficial veneer of Christianity—and in particular, that native names and locations were replaced by borrowings from the Bible, in a process he came to call "guerrilla syncretism."

If one of the ancient mysteries survived the coming of Christianity, the same thing would have happened to it. It would consist today of a handful of garbled traditions and teachings mixed up with a great many borrowings from the surrounding culture. This is exactly what we find when we look at the Master Mason degree, the central ritual of Freemasonry.

---

31. Sullivan, *The Secret of the Incas*.

The Master Mason degree centers on the death of Hiram Abiff, the son of a widow, who was supposedly the master builder of King Solomon's temple. In the legend recounted in Masonic ritual, three workmen who wanted to extract the secrets of a master mason from Hiram ambushed him in the half-completed temple one day. Each was armed with a different weapon, and each of them struck Hiram, the third fatally. They then buried his body in a hidden place, where it was later discovered, and the secrets communicated to each newly initiated Master Mason were revealed at the discovery of the grave.

Speculations concerning the origins of the Master Mason degree have covered a vast amount of territory. The great difficulty these speculations have always had to overcome is that the story of Hiram Abiff does not come from the Bible, the source of nearly all other Masonic rituals. A person named Hiram, a brass-worker who labored on King Solomon's temple, is mentioned there, but the narrative of the assassination and rediscovery of the Widow's Son is nowhere in the Bible. Nor is the story found in the abundant Jewish legends about the building of Solomon's temple, recorded in the Talmud and elsewhere. Plenty of other sources have been proposed, but one clue—a geographical clue—has been missed.

The clue in question is that Freemasonry comes from the same area of the Scottish lowlands as the stories of Merlin Caledonius.[32] The oldest surviving Masonic lodges are in and around Edinburgh. The hereditary Grand Masters of Masons in Scotland in the late Middle Ages, the Sinclair family, had their home in Roslin, south of Edinburgh, and the famous Rosslyn Chapel, with its links to medieval Masonry and the Knights Templar, is in the same area. Merlin's old refuge on Hart Fell is only fifty miles by road from Rosslyn Chapel.

Thus it is unlikely to be accidental that the story of Hiram Abiff includes a garbled version of the threefold death of Merlin Caledonius. Just as Lailoken and Merlin were killed in three different ways, Hiram Abiff was killed by being struck three times by three different weapons. Furthermore, and crucially, the Word of a Master Mason—the secret at the center of the entire ritual—is an easily recognizable mispronunciation of the Celtic divine title Mabon, which as we've seen was closely associated with the Scottish Low-

---

32. See Stevenson, *The Origins of Freemasonry.*

lands, and with Merlin.[33] There are other important parallels between the two figures, as shown in table 2–1.

Merlin	Hiram Abiff
Had no earthly father	Was the son of a widow
Was the master-builder of Stonehenge	Was the master-builder of the Temple of Jerusalem
Advised King Arthur	Advised King Solomon
Suffered a threefold death	Suffered a threefold death
Remained alive in his grave	Communicated secrets from his grave

Table 2–1: Merlin and Hiram Abiff

It's important to remember that for something like a millennium—from the early Dark Ages until the late seventeenth century—the rituals that had started out as the mysteries of the god Moridunos were passed on only by word of mouth, in secret, and had to be adapted to changing conditions. Rituals mutate dramatically under such conditions. In her engaging account of a *Shugendō*[34] initiation in Japan, anthropologist Carmen Blacker has described how, in the ceremony she attended, certain parts of the traditional ceremony were shortened or omitted, and other practices were brought in from other sources to fill the gaps.[35] Unless extraordinary efforts are made to enforce uniformity, changes of this sort happen routinely in initiation rituals around the world and throughout recorded history.

In medieval Scotland, for similar reasons and in similar ways, the rituals of initiation once celebrated atop Hart Fell varied over the years, and the same process of erosion that reduced the once-robust faiths of the Marranos and the *Kirishitan* to half-remembered scraps had ample time to work on the mysteries of Moridunos as well. Furthermore, the constant threat of persecution from Christian authorities—for more than a millennium, worshiping

---

33. As a Freemason, I am prohibited by my obligations from writing the Word of a Master Mason here or elsewhere. Readers who are interested can find it quite readily online.

34. *Shugendō* is a shamanistic religious movement in Japan, dating from the Middle Ages, that combines Buddhist practices with the ancient Japanese faith in mountain-spirits.

35. Blacker, *The Catalpa Bow*, 208–34.

any deity other than the Christian god was a crime punishable by the death penalty in Scotland—forced overtly Pagan names and symbols in the ritual to be given suitable Christian disguises; the replacement of Merlin with an imaginary "Hiram Abiff" and the relocation of the events from Hart Fell to Temple Mount in Jerusalem are typical of the sort of "guerrilla syncretism" William Sullivan documented. All things considered, it is impressive that the Master Mason ritual still has enough resemblances to the legends and traditions surrounding Merlin that the connection can still be glimpsed.

The complicated process by which the fragmentary legacies of a mystery initiation in Dark Age Scotland ended up in the hands of the founders of modern speculative Freemasonry need not be traced here.[36] The point that matters is that the traces of the Merlin legend in the Master Mason degree provide a significant piece of evidence that mystery initiations were being practiced in Roman Britain using the stories of archaic Celtic deities as their foundation. Furthermore, they suggest that these initiations were powerful and meaningful enough that, in fragmentary and much-revised form, they are still practiced today. A modern revival of the mysteries could choose any traditional or nontraditional myth as its basis, to be sure, but for a variety of reasons—some of which will be discussed in the next chapter—I have chosen the mysteries of Moridunos for my contribution to this project.

I have not, however, focused on the version of those mysteries that was once enacted on Hart Fell. Those mysteries in a very real sense are still being practiced, in the form of the Master Mason degree of Freemasonry, and it's a basic courtesy owed to living initiatory traditions—not to mention a requirement of my obligations as a Mason—not to enact any version of its rituals outside their proper context. Fortunately, no such intrusion is required, since the other half of the Merlin tradition has no such difficulties surrounding it. The mysteries of Eleusis, Agrai, and Andania all drew on legends concerning Demeter and Persephone for their rituals, without any sense that any of them were trespassing on the rites of the others. In exactly the same way, the ceremonies in this book draw from the legends of Merlin Ambrosius and thus, in a certain sense, reflect mysteries that may once have been performed on Bryn Myrddin near Carmarthen.

---

36. These will be discussed in detail in my forthcoming book, *The Ceremony of the Grail*.

Much has changed since the days of the Roman Empire, however, and the original rituals of the mysteries are long lost. Nor do we even know enough about the technical methods used in the ancient mysteries to attempt a reconstruction. Fortunately, the traditions of ceremonial magic—rooted, as we saw in this book's first chapter, in surviving traditions closely linked with the ancient mysteries—provide an ample toolkit for that project. In the next chapter, we'll survey that tradition, in order to understand the toolkit of methods that will be central to the rituals later on in this book.

―――――――――― Chapter Three ――――――――――
The Way of Self-Initiation

A metaphor might help make sense of the process by which the magical legacies of the past are being recovered and put back into use today. Imagine for a moment that some vast and intricate machine of glass and bronze was battered to pieces by a furious mob, and the fragments smashed and trampled underfoot, so that all that remained were glittering shards scattered through the gutters and trash heaps of a great city. Imagine furthermore that every record of the machine's structure and function had been destroyed to keep anyone from figuring out how to rebuild it.

Now imagine that many years later, you learn of the machine and decide to try to put it back together again. Day after day, you prowl the streets of the city, and when you find something that might once have been a piece of it, you pick it up, take it back home with you, clean off the grime, then try to figure out how it might have fit together with the other pieces you've already gathered, and what the shape of the whole machine might originally have been.[37]

That was what the pioneering occultists of the Renaissance did with the surviving fragments of the ancient world's spirituality and magic, and that's what occultists across the Western world have been doing ever since. Now and again, overenthusiastic searchers have convinced themselves that the

―――

37. I am indebted to John Crowley's visionary novel *The Solitudes* (originally titled *Aegypt*) for this metaphor.

pieces they had collected made up the entire system—the whole machine, in terms of the metaphor I've just used—but even today we're still a long way from that goal. While the entire "machine" remains elusive, however, several of its important parts have been restored to working order.

There are also "spare parts," so to speak, that have come from other sources. Some of them were borrowed from the spiritual and magical traditions of other cultures. Others have been newly invented, or reworked to make them fit the needs of the evolving occult tradition. Some purists like to take offense at this sort of creative borrowing, but two facts need to be kept in mind. The first is that people in the ancient world loved to borrow things from other cultures, too, and also to make things up from scratch. That was how the mysteries of Mithras and Isis came to be celebrated in corners of the Roman Empire far from Persia or Egypt, the original homes of the deities these mysteries invoked. It was also how new mysteries were founded straight through the history of the ancient world, and how older mysteries came to be celebrated in new ways. While the mysteries had ancient roots, they constantly had to adapt to changing circumstances and always remained open to new ideas.

Nowadays, the same flexibility is at least as necessary as it was in ancient times. What's more, there's a critical flaw in the kind of fundamentalist thinking that insists that if it wasn't done in such and such a way in the fifth century CE, it's wrong. The problem with this is simply that we don't know enough about how it was done in the fifth century CE, and we never will. Large parts of the machine, to return to the metaphor, were melted down as scrap or crushed so thoroughly that no trace of them remains. If we can't borrow or invent new traditions and practices to replace the ones that have vanished forever, we're going to be stuck permanently with a fragment of the whole.

Thus, rediscovery and reinvention are both important parts of the work of restoring the ancient wisdom. Both these approaches have been central to Western occultism since the Renaissance, and both have been particularly important in the tradition of Western occultism in which most of my work takes place—the tradition launched on its way in the eighteenth century by the founders of the Druid Revival.

DRUIDRY AND THE MYSTERIES

The original Druids, as most people know these days, were the priests, wizards, and intellectuals of the ancient Celtic peoples of Ireland, Britain, and Gaul (the modern country of France). Nobody knows much about them now. The surviving data consists of testimonies written by a small number of Greek and Roman authors, a larger body of references in medieval Celtic literature, and a great deal of archaeological evidence that can be interpreted in many ways. One of the few things that's known about them for certain is what happened to them: the Roman Empire suppressed the Druids in Gaul and the southern two-thirds or so of Britain, and Christian missionaries and priests finished the job in northern Britain and Ireland. Since it was one of the customs of the Druids never to write down anything sacred, their teachings perished with them.

More than a thousand years later, in eighteenth-century Britain, men and women who were dissatisfied with the two religious choices on offer—dogmatic Christianity on the one hand, and an equally dogmatic scientific materialism on the other—found inspiration in what little was known about the ancient Druids. A tradition among British Druids today claims that the first modern Druid organization was founded in London in 1717, and while no documentary evidence of this original Druid order has been found, there were unquestionably Druid groups meeting in London and Wales toward the middle years of the century. Ever since, Druidry has had an active presence in Britain, and spread from there to other countries—notably the United States, which saw its first Druid organization founded in upstate New York in 1798.

The history of modern Druidry is a many-colored tapestry in which Celtic lore and legend, borrowings from other spiritual traditions, and creative innovations have all played important roles. Start with so diverse a set of raw materials and the results are going to be equally diverse. This not a disadvantage; it's a point of pride in most modern Druid groups, in fact, that no two Druids have exactly the same beliefs or do things in exactly the same way. The flexibility encouraged by this custom has allowed Druidry to absorb useful ideas and practices from an astonishingly wide range of sources and weave them into a coherent whole.

One particular borrowing is particularly relevant here. In 1887 a group of English occultists founded the Hermetic Order of the Golden Dawn, a secret organization intended to teach its initiates a complete course of occult study and practice. Like most of the occult lodges of the time, it had elaborate initiation rituals that drew heavily from the ancient mysteries as well as from a wide range of other sources. (To cite only one example out of many, the officers of a Golden Dawn temple have the same titles—Hierophant, Hiereus, Hegemon, and so on—as the chief officers of the Eleusinian mysteries in ancient Greece.)

The Golden Dawn also developed an extraordinarily detailed and effective system of magic for its initiates. It's probably necessary to take a moment here and talk about what magic is, since so many unhelpful notions have gathered around it over the years. Magic, to borrow a definition attributed to the great twentieth-century British occultist Dion Fortune, is "the art and science of causing changes in consciousness in accordance with will." The tools of magic—the words and gestures that make up magical ritual, the incense and candles that play roles in setting the scene, the robes and wands and other working tools of the operative magician—are so many means of focusing and redirecting the human mind so that it comes into contact with the hidden powers of the cosmos. Some systems of magic are relatively simple, others are more complicated, and the one the Golden Dawn pieced together out of the magical traditions of the Renaissance was among the most elaborate and effective of them all.

Unfortunately, like many more recent magical groups, the Golden Dawn was much better at teaching occultism and performing rituals than managing its own internal politics. Beginning in 1900, after a long series of poorly handled disputes, the order blew itself to smithereens in a cascade of vicious power struggles, and bitter quarrels among the fragments made life difficult for everyone in that end of the British occult scene for several decades thereafter.

It so happened that just then, the Druid scene in Britain was going through a relatively placid period in its history, and it also happened that a significant number of Golden Dawn initiates were interested in Celtic traditions. The result was predictable: a great many people who fled the Golden Dawn because of the poisonous internal politics of the order's final days ended up becoming members of various Druid orders instead—and brought with them the entire toolkit of Golden Dawn magic.

During the years between the two World Wars, accordingly, there sprang up a series of hybrid orders working various fusions of Druidry and the Golden Dawn. The Ancient Order of Druid Hermetists, the Cabbalistic Order of Druids, the Nuada Temple of the Golden Dawn, and several other similar organizations thrived during this period,[38] and worked out their own rituals of initiation and their own magical practices using blendings of the two traditions.

The magical syntheses created during those years apparently didn't survive the shifts in countercultural fashion that followed the end of the Second World War. That was why, as I discussed in the introduction to my book *The Celtic Golden Dawn*, I set out to recover what was lost by reverse engineering an entire system of Druidical Golden Dawn magic from scratch. As a longtime student and practitioner of the Golden Dawn tradition, as well as a Druid who had completed the full course of initiations in three different Druid orders, I was tolerably well prepared for the task, and the system of magic and initiation I created has gone on to attract its share of students and practitioners since *The Celtic Golden Dawn* saw print.

The possibilities opened up by the reinvention of Druidical Golden Dawn magic aren't limited to those I explored in the pages of *The Celtic Golden Dawn*, however. Several years after I finished the experimental work that resulted in that book, I realized that the techniques I had developed could be put to work reviving the mysteries of Merlin.

It's probably necessary to state in so many words that the rituals, meditations, and other practices that will be presented in the chapters that follow are not the same as the ones that were practiced on Bryn Myrddin in the waning years of Roman Britain. The mysteries of that time are lost forever. Even if somehow it became possible to recover the words and ritual actions that once made up the mysteries of the god Moridunos, for that matter, their meanings have passed beyond recovery. Like all meanings, spiritual and otherwise, they unfold from a context in which language, culture, and history all take part. No one alive today can possibly experience the world in the same way as a Roman Briton of the fifth century CE, and for exactly the same reason—even if the ancient mysteries of Moridunos were available in their original form—

---

38. See Richardson and Hughes, *Ancient Magicks for a New Age*, for an account of one such group.

no one alive today could possibly experience those mysteries in the same way that a Roman Briton would have done in the fifth century CE.

Times change, and so do the mysteries. The Eleusinian mysteries themselves underwent countless changes, major and minor, over the period of more than a thousand years that they were celebrated. The transformations that apparently turned the mysteries of Merlin Caledonius into the Master Mason degree of modern Freemasonry are, as we've seen, far from unusual in the history of initiatory rites. What's more, just as there were many different mysteries in ancient Greece that centered on the myth of Demeter and Persephone, using different rituals to do so, the mysteries of Merlin set out in this book are only one of many possibilities. In the work of initiation, there's no such thing as "only one right way."

The rituals that follow, therefore, make use unapologetically of the system of Druidical ceremonial magic I reverse engineered for my book *The Celtic Golden Dawn*. They also make use of another entirely modern tradition—the custom of celebrating the festivals of the modern Pagan eightfold year-wheel.

†HE STATIONS OF THE YEAR

The eightfold year-wheel is, among other things, a fine example of the sort of inspired invention that helped create the ancient mysteries, and is helping to refound them today. Despite claims widely circulated in an older generation of Neopagan books and teachings, the year-wheel isn't an ancient tradition. According to widespread oral recollections in the British Druid scene, in fact, it was invented in a London pub around 1952 by two men, Gerald Gardner and Ross Nichols, over a couple of pints of good brown ale.

Gerald Gardner, as most readers of this book will doubtless be aware, was the central figure in the creation of modern Wicca, the man who wove a diverse assortment of fragments from many sources into the most widespread Pagan religion of the late twentieth century, and inspired many thousands of other people to ring their own changes on the themes he popularized. In 1952 his creation, then called Wica, was still very much in its formative years, and at that time it celebrated four seasonal festivals: Samhain (November 1), Candlemas (February 2), Beltane (May 1), and Lammas (August 1), which Gardner had borrowed from medieval Irish lore.

Ross Nichols, a less famous figure today, was equally influential in the London occult scene at that time. A poet and painter of considerable talent and a frequent contributor to occult periodicals, he was an important member of the British Druid movement and went on to become the most influential writer and teacher in twentieth-century Druidry. His epochal 1946 essay *The Cosmic Shape*,[39] which called for the revival of the ancient mysteries as a way to bring modern industrial humanity back into relationship with the cycles of nature, had an immense influence on the first generation of the Neopagan revival.

As we've already seen, Druidry as it now exists is a modern invention rather than an ancient tradition, but "modern" is a relative term. By the time Nichols was initiated into the Druid Order of the Universal Bond, one of the premier British Druid orders at that time, the Druid Revival had more than two centuries of history behind it and offered students a wealth of ritual and lore. At that time most Druids celebrated four seasonal festivals: the two solstices (which occur around June 21 and December 21 each year) and the two equinoxes (around March 21 and September 22 each year).

Exactly what inspired these two men to combine the calendars of their respective traditions is anyone's guess, but that was what happened. Wica, soon to be renamed Wicca, added the solstices and equinoxes to its ritual calendar, and when Nichols founded a Druid order of his own in 1964, the Order of Bards Ovates and Druids (OBOD), he added Samhain, Imbolc (another name for Candlemas), Beltane, and Lughnasadh (another name for Lammas) to the Druid ritual calendar. The result was the calendar shown in table 3–1. Over the decades that followed, the same eightfold cycle of celebrations became standard in most modern Pagan traditions. Since it was a common habit in twentieth-century Neopaganism to give innovations a veneer of respectability by backdating them to the dawn of time, many Pagan writers and teachers proceeded to claim that the eightfold wheel of the year dated from ancient times, and for a while that belief was very nearly an article of faith among many people in the Neopagan scene.

---

39. In Nichols and Kirkup, *The Cosmic Shape*.

Approximate Date*	Current Neopagan Name	Traditional Welsh Name**
1. December 21	Yule	Alban Arthan
2. February 2	Imbolc	Calan Myri
3. March 21	Ostara	Alban Eilir
4. May 1	Beltane	Calan Mai
5. June 21	Litha	Alban Hefin
6. August 1	Lammas	Calan Gwyngalaf
7. September 22	Mabon	Alban Elfed
8. November 1	Samhain	Calan Tachwedd

* In the Northern Hemisphere.

** For a small country, Wales has an impressive amount of local and regional diversity, and there are several traditional Welsh names for each of these days. I have chosen the specific set used in one of the Druid traditions into which I have been initiated.

Table 3–1: The Stations of the Eightfold Year-Wheel

It so happens that plenty of ancient Pagan calendars survive from various corners of the Europe and the world, and the eightfold wheel of the year can't be found in any of them. That's a matter of simple fact. That said, the mere fact that the eightfold wheel of the year isn't ancient doesn't make it wrong. As already noted, innovation has a necessary place in any spiritual tradition, especially when that tradition has been interrupted by history and is still being reinvented for a new era. A set of eight festivals set at roughly equal points around the cycle of the seasons has turned out to be extremely well-suited to the purposes of Pagan nature worship, and that is all the justification it needs.

In the usual way of things, the eightfold year-wheel has picked up an extensive body of symbolism in the traditions that use it. In modern American eclectic Wicca, the most widely practiced Pagan faith here in the United States, that symbolism includes specific details such as the association of Imbolc with the birth of lambs and of Lammas with the baking of the first loaf of bread from the new harvest. There's nothing wrong with these, but such symbols vary from one tradition to another. In Druidry, for example, Imbolc is often celebrated as a festival of light and water without reference to lambing, while celebrations of Lughnasadh (Lammas) focus on the rolling of a flaming wheel in celebration of the sun's temporary triumph over the gathering forces of the waning year. Other traditions use yet other symbols.

Partly this diversity reflects the fact that the seasonal cycle follows different patterns in different parts of the world, and partly it's because different magical and religious traditions choose to emphasize different aspects of the seasons in their rites. The cycle of the year-wheel is rooted in the common patterns of astronomy—the solstices and equinoxes, which anchor the cycle, are defined by the movement of the sun against the background of the stars—but the climate and ecology of different parts of the world, not to mention the cultural and spiritual orientations of different traditions, express that astronomical cycle in different ways.

What makes this relevant to our present purpose is that the eightfold wheel of the year need not be limited to the celebration of the seasons. It can also be a framework for a process of self-initiation. Just as Pagans in late classical Athens used to celebrate the mysteries of Attis and the Great Mother every spring and the mysteries of Demeter and Persephone every autumn, a modern mystery working can place different initiations around the wheel of the year to achieve the same goals of spiritual awakening. That is what I have done in this book.

The revived mysteries of Merlin presented here thus comprise eight ceremonies around the cycle of the year—the eight rituals of Merlin's Wheel. Though I've included ways to link these ceremonies to the cycle of the seasons, in whatever way that cycle expresses itself wherever you live, the rituals as such aren't keyed to any one version of the seasonal cycle. Instead, they link the cycle of the year to the human life cycle as reflected in one version of the mythic life of Merlin. This makes them just as relevant to the year as experienced in California, Alabama, Australia, or Brazil as to lowland Scotland or southern Wales, or, for that matter, the seasonal cycle I experience in my home in Rhode Island. As we'll see, it also allows these rites to be practiced alongside other rituals that celebrate the cycle of the year without any confusion of symbols, and it opens the door to a fusion between the eightfold year-wheel and the ancient mystical and magical diagram known as the Tree of Life.

†ʜᴇ Dʀᴜɪᴅ †ʀᴇᴇ ᴏꜰ Lɪꜰᴇ

No one today knows what symbolic patterns the hierophants of the Eleusinian mysteries might have used to understand the way that their rites awakened the inner lives of the *mystai* and *epoptai* who came to Eleusis each year. We do know that Pythagoras, one of the founders of ancient Greek philosophy and an initiate of many of the mysteries celebrated in his time, taught his students to make sense of the universe and themselves using a pattern of ten points, or circles, called the Tetractys.

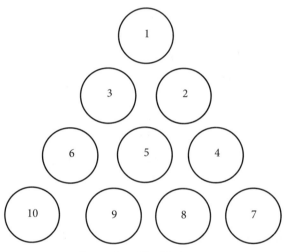

Figure 3–1: The Tetractys

Pythagoras lived in the sixth century BCE, when ancient Greece was emerging from its own medieval period and beginning to develop its own unique visions of philosophy and spirituality. Over the centuries that followed, the basic idea of the Tetractys was expanded and transformed in many ways and taken up by a wide range of spiritual traditions across the ancient world. Eventually, as a result of this process, it gave rise to the more familiar tenfold pattern known ever since as the Tree of Life.

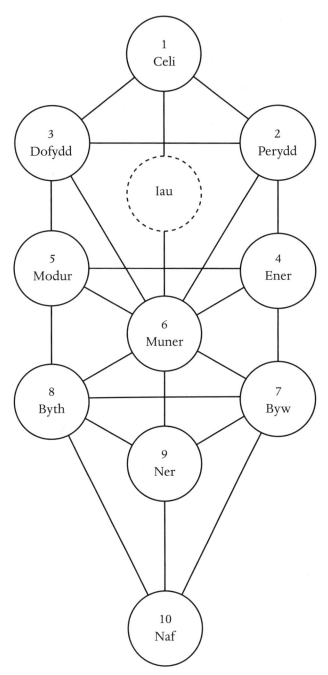

Figure 3–2: The Tree of Life

The Tree of Life is the great symbolic glyph of Western occult wisdom, a pattern of ten spheres and twenty-two paths that sets out the inner structure of the universe and the individual—in the language of traditional occultism, the macrocosm (great universe) and the microcosm (small universe). The version of the Tree of Life most often seen in modern magical literature comes from the Jewish tradition, which borrowed it from Gnostic sources in the early Middle Ages.[40] Long before it found its way into Judaism, though, the Tree of Life diagram was described in the writings of the Pagan author Celsus and his Christian opponent Origen, and a version of it, the *Wu Chi Tu*, found its way into Chinese mystical literature a century before the Tree of Life first appears in Jewish Kabbalahistic writings. We are dealing here with a very ancient and widespread symbol, one that has found its way into many traditions across the millennia.

The version of the Tree of Life worked in the rituals of Merlin's Wheel uses, as names for the ten spheres of the Tree and the unnumbered point between the third and fourth spheres, eleven traditional titles of the Divine found in *Barddas*, Iolo Morganwg's great collection of Welsh Druid Revival documents.[41] (Readers who are more familiar with the Hebrew titles for the spheres may find table 3–2 useful.) The spheres are stages in the process of creation by which the world comes into being, and they are also stages in the process of redemption by which each of us can awaken into wholeness, wisdom, and power. Both these aspects are expressed in the rituals of Merlin's Wheel.

Number	Welsh name and meaning	Hebrew name and meaning
1	Celi, the Hidden	Kether, the Crown
2	Perydd, the Maker	Chokmah, Wisdom
3	Dofydd, the Tamer	Binah, Understanding
(unnumbered circle)	Iau, the Yoke	Daath, Knowledge
4	Ener, the Namer	Chesed, Mercy
5	Modur, the Mover	Geburah, Severity

40. See Scholem, *The Origins of the Kabbalah*, for the Gnostic origins of the Jewish Kabbalah.
41. See Williams ab Ithel, *The Barddas of Iolo Morganwg*.

Number	Welsh name and meaning	Hebrew name and meaning
6	Muner, the Lord	Tiphareth, Beauty
7	Byw, the Living	Netzach, Victory
8	Byth, the Eternal	Hod, Glory
9	Ner, the Mighty	Yesod, the Foundation
10	Naf, the Shaper	Malkuth, the Kingdom

Table 3–2: The Spheres of the Tree of Life

Understanding the Tree of Life in its fullness is the work of more than one lifetime. Fortunately it's possible to work the rituals of Merlin's Wheel with a very basic understanding of it! To begin with, the spheres aren't other worlds or alternate dimensions of existence; they're principles present in everything that exists. Take yourself as an example—after all, you know yourself more thoroughly than anything else. Your material body, the structure of bones and muscles and organs that gives you your foothold in the world of matter, is the Naf, the tenth sphere, of your individual Tree of Life. Materialists like to think of the material body as the whole individual human being; practitioners of magical spirituality, on the other hand, recognize it as a small portion of the whole.

Closest to the material body is the Ner of yourself, the vital body, which is composed of the life force: the subtle vitalizing energy called *qi* in Chinese, *ki* in Japanese, *prana* in Sanskrit, *pneuma* in ancient Greek, *ruach* in Hebrew, and so on.[42] (In Welsh Druid tradition it's called *nwyfre*, pronounced "NOO-iv-ruh.") Alongside the vital body is the lower mind, the Byth of yourself, which receives and processes the messages of the physical senses, and the emotional self, the Byw of yourself, which experiences feelings. These four make up the lower self, the parts of the self that we have in common with the animals.

The three parts of yourself further up comprise the higher self, the distinctively human part of you. The Muner of you is thought; the Modur of you is will; and the Ener of you is memory. Most of us have these only in partial

---

42. It's an interesting fact that the only languages on Earth that don't have a common word for this basic human reality belong to modern Western industrial societies.

and occasional forms; human beings who develop any of them in an unusual degree are called geniuses; human beings who learn how to use all three of these capacities fully are ready to go on to another mode of being.

Finally, the three highest parts of yourself are the threefold spirit, the part of you that exists eternally. The Celi of yourself is your spiritual self; the Perydd of yourself is the spiritual self's will, or capacities for action; and the Dofydd of yourself is the spiritual self's understanding, or capacities for perception. They connect to the higher self through the Iau of yourself, which is intuition.

Apply the same principles to anything else and you have a basic sense of the spheres of the tree. In everything there's a spiritual essence; that's Celi. There's an inner capacity for will and action; that's Perydd. There's an inner capacity for understanding and experience; that's Dofydd. There's a link between these spiritual essences and their manifestation in space and time; that's Iau. There are capacities for order, for change, and for knowledge; those are Ener, Modur, and Muner. Finally, there are feelings, perceptions, life, and physical existence: those are the four lowest spheres.

The Tree of Life has potentials that haven't yet been developed as far as they can be, and some of those unfold from its relationship to the wheel of the year. Ten spheres make up the Tree, of course, and the year has eight festivals, but an important detail of magical teaching makes it easy to relate them to one another. The three highest spheres of the Tree of Life—Celi, Perydd, and Dofydd, in the version of the Tree used here—are spiritual realities outside the reach of our present level of human consciousness. Between the three higher and seven lower spheres of the Tree lies a boundary or barrier; traditional Cabalistic writings refer to it as the Abyss, while the Druidical Cabala sees it as the dividing line between the three roots of the Tree, hidden from our sight in the soil of the Unmanifest, and the seven branches of the Tree, which rise out of that soil into our awareness.

The three highest spheres therefore play no direct role in the kind of ritual work discussed in this book. We can know them only indirectly, through their effects on ourselves, or other things in the universe—and those effects act through the unnumbered point, Iau, the reflection of the three highest spheres that shape the seven lower spheres. For practical purposes, therefore, eight powers—seven of the ten spheres and Iau—make up the palette of energies we have to work with in ceremonial magic, and each of these corresponds to one of the festivals, as shown in table 3–3 below.

Date	Festival	Sphere(s)
December 21	Alban Arthan	Naf, the tenth sphere
February 2	Calan Myri	Ner, the ninth sphere
March 21	Alban Eilir	Byth, the eighth sphere
May 1	Calan Mai	Byw, the seventh sphere
June 21	Alban Hefin	Muner, the sixth sphere
August 1	Calan Gwyngalaf	Modur, the fifth sphere
September 22	Alban Elfed	Ener, the fourth sphere
November 1	Calan Tachwedd	Iau, the unnumbered point

Table 3–3: The Festivals and the Spheres

The Spheres and Their Deities

Each of the spheres of the Tree and the festivals of the year-wheel also corresponds to one of the deities traditionally invoked by the Druid Revival, and some basic familiarity with these deities and their symbolism will be helpful in working with the ceremonies of Merlin's Wheel. In the paragraphs below, we'll survey this lore, along with the basic concepts of the spheres of the Tree of Life and the festivals of the year-wheel as they are understood in the Druid Revival tradition.

Alban Arthan/Naf: Olwen

Naf, the tenth sphere of the Tree, is the realm of material existence, where the light of spirit reaches its lowest ebb; it corresponds to the ground center in the human body, which is between the feet when you are standing upright, and also to the element of earth. In much the same way, the winter solstice is the point of the annual cycle at which the sun has reached its lowest point in the southern sky. It's not accidental that many gods have their traditional birthday around this time of year, for the imagery of light and new life kindling in the darkness fits the energies of the seasons well.

The deity assigned to this festival is Olwen of the White Track—"white track" is the meaning of her name in Welsh—who appears in the story of Culhwch and Olwen in the *Mabinogion*, the great treasury of Welsh traditional legend. While her apparent role in the story is that of a human princess, she is the daughter of a magical giant, Yspaddaden Penkawr (literally, "Hawthorn, Chief of the Giants"), and four white flowers spring up wherever she steps. In the Druid Revival traditions she is recognized as the maiden goddess of the waxing year, whose "footprints" are the first flowers that bloom amid the melting snow to proclaim the approach of spring. The *Mabinogion* describes her as blonde and pale-skinned, dressed in a gown of flame-red silk. Around her neck is a torque of gold set with pearls and rubies.

Calan Myri/Ner: Coel or Sul

The ninth sphere of the Tree of Life, Ner the Mighty, is the realm of the life force, of the tides of subtle substance that unite all living things. It corresponds to the genital center in the human body, and to the element of water. Its correspondence in the wheel of the year is Calan Myri, the first festival of the waxing year, a celebration of light and water that honors the lengthening days and the first stirrings of life in the newborn year.

As the sphere corresponding to reproduction and sexuality, Ner has two deities assigned to it in Druid lore, a god and a goddess, representing the polarization of sexual energies into masculine and feminine. The god Coel is dimly remembered in the children's rhyme:

Old King Cole was a merry old soul
And a merry old soul was he ...

The god of the life force, he is the patron of woodlands and wild animals. His name is the Welsh word for "faith" or "trust." In modern Druid lore he is envisioned as a massively built man with wild hair and beard, dressed as a huntsman in russet and dark brown, with stag's antlers rising from his head.

The goddess Sul is also a deity of the life force, associated with the healing springs at Bath in England, where the Romans revered her as Sulis Minerva. Her name is derived from an ancient word for the sun. The daughter of the year-god Belinus, she rules the threefold fire—the sun, the heat within the earth, and the fire in the hearth—and is the divine patron of healing and of all domestic crafts. Modern Druid lore pictures her as an adult woman with golden hair, wearing a white gown, a red cloak, and golden ornaments.

Alban Eilir/Byth: Mabon[43]

The eighth sphere of the Tree of Life is Byth the Eternal, the realm of sensation and perception, which corresponds to the element of air and the navel center in the human body. It corresponding festival is Alban Eilir, the spring equinox, which marks the renewal of vegetation and the triumph of light over darkness.

As explained in chapter 2, the name Mabon simply means "The Son." As Mabon, son of Modron ("Son, son of Mother"), he plays an enigmatic role in the story of Culhwch and Olwen in the *Mabinogion*, and some scholars believe that the word "Mabinogion" itself comes from an archaic Welsh phrase meaning something like "tales of the Mabon." According to the tale, Mabon was taken from his mother when he was three days old, and he remained a prisoner until the warriors of Arthur, guided by the oldest animals in the world, came to rescue him. In modern Druid lore he is the eternal child, at once the god of youth and the guardian of a timeless wisdom. He may be pictured as a child with dark hair and bright eyes, barefoot and bareheaded, and dressed only in a plain sleeveless tunic of unbleached cloth.

Calan Mai/Byw: Elen

Byw the Living, the seventh sphere of the Tree of Life, is the realm of emotion and intuition; it corresponds to the solar plexus center in the human body, and to the element of fire. Its festival is Calan Mai, a festival of flowers and greenery, when spring has come into its own and the natural world is aflame with the verdant fire of growth.

Its deity is Elen of the Roads. Like Olwen, Elen appears in humanized form in one of the stories from the *Mabinogion*, "The Dream of Macsen Wledig." Her name is a Welsh word for "angel" or "female spirit." In her divine form she is the goddess of love, and also of dawn and dusk, the times of day when her planet Venus appears as the morning and evening star. Finally, she is the divine power ruling over the old straight tracks, the ancient network of

---

43. Some modern American Wiccan traditions associate Mabon with the autumn equinox. I am not a Wiccan and don't pretend to understand the reasoning behind this attribution; in the Druid Revival traditions, the Mabon as a young deity is primarily a springtime god, and also features in some rituals of Lughnasadh/Calan Gwyngalaf as a figure representing masculine energy to balance the feminine energy of Imbolc/Calan Myri.

energy paths and sacred sites often described (and too often misunderstood) as "ley lines." The *Mabinogion* describes her as auburn-haired and beautiful, dressed in a white gown with a surcoat and mantle of gold brocade, with a broach, belt, and jeweled hair band of gold.

Alban Hefin/Muner: Esus

The blazing heart of the Tree of Life, Muner is the sixth sphere and stands at the midpoint between Celi, the hidden spirit, and Naf, the material world. It corresponds to the heart center in the human body and the first aspect of the element of spirit, Spirit Within. In the same way, Alban Hefin, the summer solstice, stands at the midpoint of the year between one winter solstice and the next. It is traditionally celebrated by Druids with a vigil from midnight to dawn, a ceremony to welcome the midsummer sunrise, then—after a few hours of sleep!—music, poetry, and feasting when the sun stands high in the heavens at noon.

The chief of tree-spirits, guardian of green things, and emissary of the great Druid god Hu the Mighty, Esus takes his title ("Lord" in the old Celtic language) from an ancient Gaulish deity of whom very little is known. His role as a god of the modern Druid Revival tradition is largely a result of visionary experience among nineteenth- and twentieth-century Druids. He is pictured in Druid lore as a lean brown man of indeterminate age who sits perched in the first fork of the sacred oak. His garments of brown and green look like bark and leaves; his hands are long, brown, and strong as roots, and his eyes are very bright.

Calan Gwyngalaf/Modur: Taranis

Modur is the great center of dynamism and force on the Tree of Life; it corresponds to the throat center in the human body, where the power of the voice has its central focus, and to the second aspect of the element of spirit, Spirit Below. Its festival is Calan Gwyngalaf, when the summer heat is strongest and the sun does battle each day with the gathering forces of the year's waning half.

The thunder god of the ancient Celts, Taranis ("He of the Lightning") has close equivalents all through Indo-European mythologies; his name and character are akin to the Norse Thor, Old English Thunor, Lithuanian

Perkunas, Russian Perun, and many others of the same kind. He may be pictured as a man of immense strength with rippling muscles and red-gold hair and beard, bare to the waist and dressed below that in leather trews (trousers going to just below the knees) and sturdy boots. Like his equivalents in related mythologies, he wields a mighty hammer.

Alban Elfed/Ener: Belinus

The fourth sphere of the Tree of Life, Ener is the sphere of space and expansion; the highest of the seven lower spheres, it accordingly marks the highest level of being, according to Druid philosophy, to which human beings and other created entities can aspire. It corresponds to the brow center in the human body and to the third aspect of the element of spirit, Spirit Above. Its festival is Alban Elfed, the middle of the harvest in the temperate zone, when the bounty of the earth is most evident.

The year-god who dies and is reborn at the winter solstice, Belinus ("The Shining One") is the lord of the seasonal cycle in the Druid Revival tradition; the numerical value of the Greek letters that form his name, βηλενός, add up to 365, the number of days in a solar year.[44] In modern Druid lore, he traces out the cycle of the seasons as he passes through the stages of his journey from pale infant to strong young god, to lover and mate of the living earth, to king, to sacrifice, to pale corpse laid out on the bier of the sky. In his role as lord of Alban Elfed, he may be pictured as a strong and virile man of middle years with golden hair and beard, wearing a red tunic and cloak ornamented with gold, and carrying a long spear and a golden shield.

Calan Tachwedd/Iau: Ceridwen

Iau, as already noted, is not a sphere of the Tree of Life, but a link or point of contact between the three higher spheres and the seven lower spheres. It corresponds to the crown center in the human body and to the divine reality that lies above the element of spirit. Its festival of Calan Tachwedd, called Samhain by the Irish, is the point in the annual cycles at which the barriers between this world and the otherworld are thinnest, the harvest is over, and the earth sinks into its winter sleep.

---

44. Julius Caesar wrote that the ancient Gauls used Greek letters for writing, so the numerical value of the name is unlikely to be accidental.

The goddess of the moon, Ceridwen—her name in Welsh means "bent woman," and refers to the shape Americans call "the man in the moon" and Welsh tradition pictures as an old woman stooping over a cauldron—is the keeper of the secrets of Druid initiation. She plays a central role in the legend of the great Druid bard Taliesin. In that story she has three children: a daughter named Creirwy ("Heron's Egg"), a son named Morfran ("Sea Raven"), and another son named Afagddu ("Complete Darkness"). These are the different forms of the moon: Creirwy as the full, Morfran as the crescent, and Afagddu as the days close to the new moon when no sign of the moon can be seen at all. She is pictured in modern Druid lore as an old woman with moon-white hair, clad in heavy garments of brown and black, stirring a steaming cauldron.

It's probably necessary, while talking about gods and goddesses, to clarify a point that sometimes gets confused in modern magical literature. The polytheist faiths of the ancient world were by and large very clear about the difference between human beings and deities. Some people of unusual holiness and power, as we have seen, came to be recognized after their deaths as incarnations of deities, or as minor deities in their own right. This was the exception that proved the rule, though, and was subject to stringent tests—in both Athens and Rome, for example, before divine honors could be conferred on any dead person, the legislature had to investigate the case and pass a bill to that effect. (The Roman Catholic process by which saints are investigated and proclaimed is descended from the Roman version of this custom.)

The point I hope to make here can be put even more plainly. You are not a god or a goddess, and practicing rituals of self-initiation will not make you one. The goal of initiation as the ancient mysteries practiced it, and as the rituals of Merlin's Wheel confer it today, is to come into a closer relationship with the transcendent spiritual realities at the center of being, not to elbow those realities aside so that your ego can take their place.

Furthermore—and this is crucial—these rituals will not turn you into Merlin, or make you a priest or priestess of the god Moridunos, or give you any other special status you can parade in front of your friends. Their purpose is to attune you with the profound spiritual forces that are expressed through the traditional stories of Merlin, which "never happened but always are," and to participate in the energies corresponding to eight Celtic deities who correspond in a subtle but real manner to the eight stations of the year. That process of attunement and participation will lead to greater insight and personal growth, just as a similar process gave the same gifts to the *mystai* and *epoptai* of the Eleusinian mysteries.

Initiation and Self-Initiation

In the course of the year, according to the scheme of eight festivals just outlined, it's possible to work with each stage of the ancient legends of Merlin in turn, and in the process, to awaken each of the spheres of the Tree of Life accessible to human consciousness in a systematic manner. This adds a new and important dimension to the ancient custom of working mystery rituals at intervals around the cycle of the year, and makes it possible for those rituals to function as the keynotes in an effective system of self-initiation.

The origins of the ancient mysteries are lost in antiquity, but some modern scholars have suggested that they began with seasonal reenactments of a sacred story. Over time, the process by which each new generation came to participate in those rites took on greater and greater importance, until the mysteries served primarily as a way of initiation and the purely seasonal elements faded into the background. Even after the mysteries had been reworked so they could be done in private houses, they remained a group practice, something done by *epoptai* for the benefit of *mystai*. The idea of self-initiation only emerged very late, as the ancient world approached its end and initiates of the mysteries searched for ways to preserve their rites and teachings in the face of Christian persecution.

Yet emerge it did, and several surviving rituals show how self-initiation was practiced in ancient times. Among the many rituals preserved in the Greek magical papyri found in Egypt, for example, is a liturgy of Mithras adapted for solitary use. The great scholar of religions Albrecht Dieterich argued that this ritual derives from the highest of the seven degrees of Mithraic initiation. Whether or not this is the case, it shows that the mysteries of Mithras had been adapted by the third century CE to use the technical methods of ancient ceremonial magic for the purpose of self-initiation.[45]

An equally revealing ritual of self-initiation can be found in the *Picatrix*. Derived from the austere and intellectual mysteries of Hermes Trismegistus, this ritual is intended to awaken the Perfect Nature or higher self of the initiate. It was performed once each year at a day and time when the moon was in the first degree of Aries. The practitioner made offerings of wine, oil, and incense, faced east, chanted the four secret names of Perfect Nature, and recited an invocation—all of these, of course, are technical methods that saw much use in the ceremonial magic of the time.[46] Elsewhere in the *Picatrix*, similar rituals allowed mages to initiate themselves into the mysteries of the planetary gods.

Nowadays religious persecution is no longer a problem in most of the world's industrial nations, and for several centuries now, initiation rituals of various kinds have again been performed by groups of experienced practitioners for new initiates. Self-initiation, however, remains a valid approach, and for many people it remains the best of the available options. Not everyone, after all, lives within easy commuting distance of a group that performs one of the modern magical initiatory systems, or can find the free time and the money to travel to such a group on a regular basis and help support its work.

Nearly everyone, however, can find the time to carry out a program of self-initiation in their off hours. This was why, when I reconstructed the system of Druidical ceremonial magic set out in my book *The Celtic Golden Dawn*, I designed it around a process of self-initiation. In that process, each student proceeds at his or her own pace through the three traditional grades of Ovate, Bard, and Druid, using the daily practice of ritual, meditation, and divination to accomplish the work of awakening the magical potentials of the self.

The mysteries in ancient times, however, were not restricted to those few who intended to take up the demanding spiritual disciplines of ceremonial magic. The procession of *mystai* that went to Eleusis in the month of Boedromion each year included men and women from every walk of life. Some of them meant to turn initiation in the mysteries into the keynote of a life

---

45. The ritual has been published in translation many times and can be found in full in Meyer, *The Ancient Mysteries*, 211–21.

46. The full text is given in Greer and Warnock, *Picatrix*, 150–51.

devoted to the search for wisdom, but many others made room for the mysteries as part of more ordinary ways of living. The same was true of most of the ancient mysteries, and it can be just as true of their modern equivalents.

Self-initiation in the mysteries of Merlin's Wheel does require a little more knowledge of ritual practice than it would have taken to be initiated into the Eleusinian mysteries, or for that matter the mysteries of Moridunos in late Roman Britain. After all, no one else is there to perform the ritual for you! In the next chapter, we'll walk step by step through the rituals that will be needed for the eight ceremonies of Merlin's Wheel.

One core advantage in self-initiation is that the newcomer to the work can start with a simple form of initiation, work at that level for a period, then use the skills developed at that stage of the work to add higher and deeper dimensions to the practice if he or she wishes to do so. The traditions of the Druid Revival make this easy by dividing the initiatory process into the three grades of Ovate, Bard, and Druid.

In traditional Druidry, the first or Ovate grade is the stage of beginnings, and its symbolic color is green, emblematic of the first green shoots of springtime growth. The second or Bardic grade is the stage of growth and development, of moving into higher and deeper levels of experience, and its symbolic color is the blue of sky and sea, emblematic of the heights and the depths. The third or Druid grade is the stage of mastery, and its symbolic color is white, emblematic of the shining light in which all colors are united.[47]

In the system of rituals presented in this book, the three grades are used as a basis for three Circles, which are three ways that the eight rituals of Merlin's Wheel can be practiced. The Ovate Circle rituals are designed for complete beginners who have no previous experience of ceremonial magic, Druidical or otherwise. By the time you finish working through all eight ceremonies in their simplified Ovate form, you'll be ready to proceed to the next set of rituals, those of the Bardic Circle, which have been expanded considerably by the

---

47. This order of grades—Ovate, Bard, Druid—was standard in nineteenth- and early twentieth-century Druid traditions. Ross Nichols, the founder of the Order of Bards Ovates and Druids (OBOD), deliberately changed this in his organization, putting the Bardic grade first to emphasize the poetic and artistic side of the tradition. As OBOD is the largest and most influential Druid order in the world today, Nichols' order of the grades is the most common in contemporary Druidry; I prefer, however, to use the older approach.

addition of further ceremonial and meditative tools. A year spent working the Bardic Grade rituals, in turn, will prepare you to go on to the more complex and powerful rituals of the Druid Circle. If you come to this work as a beginner, it will take three years of steady work before you can perform the full set of eight rituals in their complete form—but those three years will also initiate you thoroughly into the mysteries of Merlin's Wheel and take you far along the path of self-initiation more generally.

If you come to these mysteries with experience in other magical traditions, you'll find it useful to read through the rituals that follow and compare the work that's needed to perform them to your existing skill set. If you have any doubts about the fit between your training and the work of Merlin's Wheel, it's probably wisest to start with the Ovate Circle rituals and work up from there—even if nearly all of the work is familiar to you, every initiate needs a refresher course in the basics now and then.

Finally, if you're already a student of the system of Druidical ceremonial magic presented in my book *The Celtic Golden Dawn*, much of what follows will already be familiar to you—though there's some new material to master here as well. The fine details of combining the work of Merlin's Wheel with the broader training system of *The Celtic Golden Dawn* are covered in chapter 8.

———— CHAPTER FOUR ————
RITUALS AND MEDITATIONS

R oss Nichols, the most significant Druid teacher and writer of the twentieth century, defined ritual memorably in a single crisp phrase: "Ritual is poetry in the world of acts."[48] Just as a well-crafted poem uses the tools of language to help the reader experience something of the mood or experience that inspired it, a well-crafted magical ritual uses a much broader set of tools—words, gestures, physical props, and mental imagery—to help the ritualist enter into different states of consciousness and come into contact with the powers and insights each of these states of consciousness has to offer.

Put another way, magical ritual is, among other things, a performing art. Like every other performing art, it takes a certain amount of practice to be able to do it well, and the more work you put into preparation and practice, the better the results will be. Unlike most performing arts, it's not done for spectators. In the rituals given in this book, you are the audience as well as the performer. That has certain advantages—among other things, you're guaranteed the best seat in the house!—but it also places certain requirements on you as performer as well as audience. To do it well, to accomplish the work of self-initiation that the rituals of Merlin's Wheel are meant to accomplish, it's important to understand what you're doing, and to practice it often enough that you don't have to fumble with half-familiar words and actions while you're doing it.

---

48. See Nichols and Kirkup, *The Cosmic Shape*, for a detailed exploration of this theme.

That's a little easier than it might otherwise be, because the ceremonies of Merlin's Wheel are assembled from a set of shorter rituals and practices, each of which has a specific magical function in the larger structure. (This sort of modular structure is standard in modern traditions of ceremonial magic.) Each of those shorter pieces can be learned and practiced by itself and then brought into the larger ritual at the appropriate point. What's more, the shorter ceremonies and practices that make up the mystery rituals of Merlin's Wheel have many other magical uses, so the work you'll need to put into learning and rehearsing them will pay off many times over as you pursue your own magical path.

As we discussed in chapter 3, each of the eight rituals can be performed at three different levels: the Ovate Circle or beginning level, the Bardic Circle or intermediate level, and the Druid Circle or advanced level. The same principle of building larger structures from smaller parts applies here as well. The ceremony you learn and perform at the Ovate level isn't discarded when you pass to the Bardic level; instead, new elements are added to the existing structure. The same thing happens as you transition to the Druid level. When you start performing the rituals on the Bardic level, in other words, the year of experience you've put into the Ovate rituals will carry over into the framework of the Bardic rituals, and by the time you get to the rituals of the Druid level, you'll already have two years of experience with some parts of the ceremony, and one year with other parts.

The Ovate Workings

These are the simplest versions of the eight rituals of Merlin's Wheel and can be performed by anyone, even a complete beginner, who is willing to learn the very basic ritual practices used at this level. Each of the Ovate rituals includes the following steps:

1. Perform the opening ritual.
2. Invoke the energies of the season with the Octagram and an invocation.
3. Read aloud the symbolic narrative of the season.
4. Meditate on the narrative and the energies of the season.

5. Release the energies of the season with the Octagram and words of thanks.

6. Perform the closing ritual.

The opening and closing rituals are also assembled from parts, and those parts are best learned one at a time, beginning with the most basic ritual action you'll need to know, the Rite of the Rays.

The Rite of the Rays

This is an opening and closing gesture, the simplest of the ritual methods taught in the system of magic used in this book. It combines gesture, voice, and imagination in a single magical act. Its purpose is to orient the self toward the divine, symbolized by the Three Rays of Light— / | \ —the Druidical symbol of creation.

The words used in the Rite of the Rays are in the Welsh language, and mean in English "Alawn, Plennydd, and Gwron, the Three Rays of Light." The three names Alawn, Plennydd, and Gwron mean "harmony," "light," and "virtue," and according to tradition, they were the names of the three original bards of the island of Britain. They also have a deeper meaning, which will be discussed a little later in this chapter.

The final word in the ritual is "Awen," which is one of the great sacred words of Druidry, filling much the same role in Druid Revival symbolism and spirituality that the famous word Om (Aum) has in Hindu and Buddhist mysticism, or the various names of God have in traditions descended from one of the monotheistic religions. Awen is the spirit of inspiration, the spiritual presence inside every being that gives insight into the depths of being. In ritual it is always pronounced as though divided into three syllables, "AH-OO-EN," with each syllable drawn out and held for the same length of time as the others.

None of these words are simply spoken, though; in the jargon of the operative mage, they are *vibrated*. This is a particular mode of speaking or chanting names, words, and phrases of power. To vibrate a word is to utter it in such a way that it produces a buzzing or tingling sensation in your body. To learn how to do this, take a vowel sound such as "ah" and draw it out, changing the way your mouth and throat shape the sound until you feel the sensation just described. Once you can do this reliably, you can proceed to learn the Rite of the Rays, which is done as follows.

First, stand straight, feet together, arms at sides, facing east. Pause, clear your mind, then visualize yourself expanding upward and outward, through the air and through space, until your body is so large that your feet rest on the earth as though on a ball a foot across; the sun is at your solar plexus, and your head is amongst the stars. Then raise your hands up from your sides in an arc above your head. Join them palm to palm, fingers and thumbs together and pointing upward. Then draw them down until your thumbs touch the center of your forehead. As you do this, visualize a ray of light descending from infinite space above you to form a star of brilliant white light above the top of your head. Vibrate the word MAE (pronounced "MY").

Second, draw down your joined hands to the level of your heart, and visualize a ray of light shining from the blazing star above your head down the midline of your body, and descending into infinite space directly below you. Vibrate the word ALAWN (pronounced "ALL-own," the last syllable rhyming with "crown").

Third, leaving your left hand at heart level, move your right hand down and to your right in an arc until it forms a diagonal line from shoulder to fingertips. The palm should finish facing forward. As you do this, visualize a ray of light shining from the star of light above your head along the line of your right arm, and descending into infinite space below and to your right. Vibrate the word PLENNYDD (pronounced "PLEN-nuth," with the "th" voiced as in "these," rather than unvoiced as in "thin").

Fourth, make an identical motion with your left hand, extending it down and to your left until it too forms a diagonal line from shoulder to fingertips. As you do this, visualize a ray of light shining from the star of light above your head along the line of your left arm, and descending into infinite space below and to your left. Vibrate the words A GWRON (pronounced "ah GOO-ron").

Fifth, cross your arms across your chest, right arm over left, with your fingertips resting on the front part of your shoulders. Visualize all three rays of light and vibrate the words Y TEYR PELYDRYN GOLEUNI (pronounced "ee TEIR pell-UD-run go-LEY-nee"). Then, in a single smooth motion, raise your elbows upward and sweep both arms up, out, and down to your sides, then bring them palm to palm at groin level and raise them to the center of your chest, turning the fingers upward and bringing the thumbs to touch your chest. Vibrate the word AWEN (pronounced "AH-OO-EN," with each of the three syllables held for an equal length of time). This completes the ritual.

Practice the Rite of the Rays daily for at least a week before going on to learn the Lesser Ritual of the Pentagram. Simple though it is, the Rite is not a mere formality. It contains a wealth of magical potential that can be understood only through practice, and time spent mastering it will not be wasted.

The Lesser Ritual of the Pentagram

This is one of the workhorse rituals of the system of magic used in this book, a basic magical practice with many applications. It is done in two forms, summoning and banishing. The summoning form clears a space of unwanted and unbalanced forces, and calls in the powers of the four elements in a balanced way. The banishing form clears the space again and returns the powers of the elements to their normal condition.

The difference between the two forms is purely a matter of how the pentagrams are traced: in the summoning ritual the pentagram is traced clockwise from the uppermost point, while in the banishing ritual it is traced counterclockwise from the same point. The summoning ritual is done at the beginning of a ceremony, the banishing ritual at the end.

This differs from the way that pentagrams are traced in the Lesser Ritual of the Pentagram as it's usually practiced, and this is quite deliberate. The standard way of tracing pentagrams in modern magical practice comes from the traditions of the Hermetic Order of the Golden Dawn and is rooted in Judeo-Christian symbolism. Thus the basic all-purpose banishing in Golden Dawn practice, and the traditions that descend from it, uses a pentagram traced from the point of earth to the point of spirit, the same gesture used to banish the element of earth. Why? Because an enduring theme of Christian teaching is the rejection of everything earthly as evil.

That attitude isn't to be found in Celtic Pagan traditions of the sort that underlie the rituals of Merlin's Wheel, nor is it present in the traditions of the Druid Revival that have shaped the magic used in this book. Instead, these see the world of matter as a place of learning and delight—not a trap from which the soul must struggle free. Thus the method for tracing the pentagrams used here does not treat the earth as something to be banished! Instead, it draws on Druid teachings about the creation and dissolution of the world at the beginning and end of the great cycles of time.

To summon the subtle energies of magic at the beginning of a rite, we bring energy down from spirit in a clockwise pattern, passing through the points of the pentagram assigned to fire, air, water, and earth in that order, and returning to spirit: the order in which *nwyfre*,[49] the life force, descended through the elemental planes in the creation of the world, according to Druid philosophy. To banish, in turn, we trace the pentagram counterclockwise from the point of spirit, through the points of earth, water, air, and fire in that order, and returning to spirit: the order in which *nwyfre* will ascend through the elemental planes at the dissolution of the world.

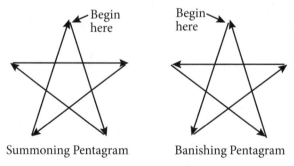

Figure 4–1: Summoning and Banishing Pentagrams

With these changes kept in mind, the Lesser Summoning Ritual of the Pentagram is performed as follows:

---

49. Pronounced "NOO-iv-ruh." Nwyfre is the Druid name for that subtle energy of life called *prana* in Sanskrit, *qi* in Chinese, and so on.

First, standing in the center of the space in which you are working, face east and perform the complete Rite of the Rays.

Second, go to the eastern quarter of the space. Using the index and middle fingers of your right hand, with the others folded under your thumb in the palm of your hand, trace a pentagram in the air in front of you in the first fashion shown in figure 4–1, starting down and to the right from the topmost point and then continuing clockwise around to the same point. The pentagram should be upright, two or three feet across, with the center around the level of your shoulder. As you trace the line, visualize the pentagram taking shape before you, as though your fingers were drawing it in a line of golden light. When you have finished, point to the center and vibrate the divine name HEU'C (pronounced "HEY'k").

Third, with your extended fingers, trace a line around the circumference of the space a quarter circle to your right, ending at the southern quarter. Visualize the line in golden light as you trace it. Trace a pentagram in the south in the same way as you did in the east, point to the center, and vibrate the divine name SULW (pronounced "SILL-w").

Fourth, repeat the process, tracing a line another quarter of the way around the circle to the west, visualizing it in golden light, and trace and visualize the pentagram as you did in the east and south. Point to the center of the pentagram and vibrate the divine name ESUS (pronounced "ESS-iss").

Fifth, repeat the process once more, tracing a line around to the north, tracing and visualizing a pentagram there, and vibrating the divine name ELEN (pronounced "ELL-enn").

Sixth, trace a line as before back around to the east, completing the circle, then return to the center and face east. Extend your arms down and out to your sides, once again taking on the posture of the Three Rays of Light. Say: "Before me the Hawk of May and the powers of air. Behind me the Salmon of Wisdom and the powers of water. To my right hand, the White Stag and the powers of fire. To my left hand, the Great Bear and the powers of earth. For about me stand the pentagrams, and upon me shine the Three Rays of Light."

As you name each of these things, visualize it as solidly and intensely as you can. You are surrounded by the elements—a springtime cloudscape to the east, a summer scene of blazing heat to the south, an autumn seascape to the west, and a forest in winter to the north—with the animal guardians visible against these backgrounds. The pentagrams and circle form a pattern like a crown surrounding you, and the Three Rays of Light shine down from the starry center of light above your head as in the Rite of the Rays.

Seventh, perform the complete Rite of the Rays as before. This completes the ritual.

The Lesser Banishing Ritual of the Pentagram is performed exactly the same way as the Summoning version, except that the pentagram is drawn the other direction, counterclockwise from the topmost point, as shown in figure 4–1.

Both these rituals should be practiced regularly so that you can do them without having to follow a script. It takes around five minutes to do each of them, so a very modest investment of practice time will be enough to learn them. The payoff from that investment, in terms of the effects you will get from the practice of the seasonal rituals, will be well worth the time spent.

Opening and Closing a Temple
The Lesser Ritual of the Pentagram is the most important step in preparing a space for the ceremonies of the mysteries of Merlin's Wheel, but it doesn't stand alone. In most systems of modern ceremonial magic, including the one used in this book, a more extensive ritual that includes the Pentagram Ritual is used to open a temple of the mysteries before the ceremony begins. Another similar ritual is used to close the temple once the ceremony is finished.

In ancient times, of course, the temples of the mysteries were exactly that: sacred buildings, as large and splendid as the local community could support, which were only used for ceremonial purposes. In the waning years of the ancient world, as religious intolerance made the public celebration of the Mysteries impossible, those who preserved the traditions downsized their facilities to match their resources, and people took to celebrating the mysteries in their own homes. The habit of celebrating the rituals of alternative religious traditions in living rooms goes back a surprisingly long way, and that is the custom we'll be following here.

The temple you will be establishing for the eight seasonal rituals, in other words, will be a convenient room indoors or a private outdoor space, which can be used for ordinary purposes on every other day of the year. The requirements are simple: a place for an altar in the center of the space, a place for a chair in the west, ample room to walk around on all sides, and privacy.

Date	Festival	Color
December 21	Alban Arthan	Brown
February 2	Calan Myri	Violet
March 21	Alban Eilir	Orange
May 1	Calan Mai	Green
June 21	Alban Hefin	Gold
August 1	Calan Gwyngalaf	Red
September 22	Alban Elfed	Blue
November 1	Calan Tachwedd	Black

Table 4–1: Colors of the Festivals

The altar can be any convenient flat-topped surface large enough to hold two bowls and three candlesticks. For best results it should rise to somewhere between your knees and your waist. The altar is covered by an altar cloth, which may be a plain unhemmed length of fabric, or something as elaborate and beautiful as your budget or your sewing skills permit. You may use a plain white altar cloth, which is standard in Druidical practice, or an altar cloth of a different color for each of the eight celebrations, as shown in table 4–1.

On the altar go three white candles in candlesticks, a bowl or small cauldron of clean water, and a bowl or small cauldron of sand, which is used for burning incense. You may use any kind of incense you prefer. If you're using stick incense, simply thrust the end of the stick into the sand, while if you're using cone incense or loose incense on charcoal, the cone or charcoal can be set on the sand.

As with the altar cloth, the candlesticks and the bowls or cauldrons can be as simple or as elaborate as you wish and can afford. They are placed on the altar as shown in figure 4–2; the cauldron or bowl on your left, as you stand at the west of the altar facing east, is for water, and the one on your right is for incense.

Figure 4–2: Arrangement of the Altar

You can also decorate the altar according to the season—for example, if you live in the northern temperate zone, you might choose holly or fir boughs in the winter, flowers in the spring, greenery in the summer, and ripe fruit or ears of grain in the autumn. If your local seasonal cycle has a different pattern, follow that pattern and choose your altar decorations accordingly. The point of the seasonal decor is not to follow a rigid symbolic scheme, but to help you link the legendary cycle of the life of Merlin in your imagination with the cycle of the year, and with the subtle cycles of your own consciousness and its awakening into greater light and life.

Finally, put a chair on the western side of the space, facing the altar. Once you have set up the space, put clean water in the water bowl or cauldron, light the incense, then sit in the chair facing the altar for a few moments to calm your mind and clear every other concern from your thoughts. All your attention should be on the ritual you are about to perform. When you are ready, stand up, go to the west side of the altar, and begin.

The opening ritual is performed as follows:

First, stand on the west side of the altar, facing east. Raise your right hand, palm facing toward the east, and say: "In the presence of the holy powers of Nature, I prepare to open this temple of the mysteries. Let peace be proclaimed with power, throughout this temple and in the hearts of all who stand herein."

Second, perform the Lesser Summoning Ritual of the Pentagram, tracing the pentagrams clockwise from the top point. Begin and end on the west side of the altar, facing east.

Third, take up the cauldron or bowl of water in both hands and raise it high above the altar. Say: "Let this temple and all within it be purified with the waters of the sacred well." Carry the cauldron to the eastern quarter of the space. Holding the cauldron in your right hand, dip the fingers of the left hand into the water, then flick droplets of water off your fingers three times—once down and to your right, once down and to your left, and once straight down. This pattern represents the Three Rays of Light / | \ .

Carry the cauldron around to the southern quarter and repeat the same action, sprinkling droplets of water three times in the same way. Proceed to the western quarter and then to the northern quarter, repeating the same action in each, so that the four quarters have been cleansed and purified with water in the sign of the Three Rays of Light. Return to the eastern quarter, completing the circle; raise the cauldron of water in both hands, and say: "The temple is purified." When this is done, return to the west side of the altar, facing east, and replace the cauldron in its proper place on the left side.

Fourth, take up the cauldron or bowl of incense in both hands, and raise it high above the altar. Say: "Let this temple and all within it be consecrated with the smoke of the sacred fire."

Next, carry the cauldron of incense to the eastern quarter of the space. Holding the cauldron in your left hand, use your right hand to wave the smoke upward from the cauldron three times—once up and to your left, once up and to your right, and once straight up. This pattern represents the Three Rays of Light in another form \ | /.

Carry the cauldron around to the southern quarter and repeat the same action, directing the incense upward three times in the same way. Proceed to the western quarter, then to the northern quarter, repeating the same action in each, so that the four quarters have been blessed and consecrated with incense in the sign of the Three Rays of Light. Return to the eastern quarter, completing the circle; raise the cauldron of incense in both hands, and say: "The temple is consecrated." When this is done, return to the west side of the altar, facing east, and replace the cauldron in its proper place on the right side.

Fifth, circumambulate the temple. This is an ancient rite, practiced in many traditions, that involves simply walking around a sacred place or object in a clockwise direction. From where you stand west of the altar, go around the north side of the altar to the east and begin to circle the altar, keeping it always on your right side. Every time you pass the east, cross your arms upon your chest, right arm over left, and bow your head, without stopping or breaking the rhythm of your pace. Circle the altar in a clockwise direction, from east to east, three full times, then circle back around to the west side of the altar and face east.

Sixth, when the circumambulation is finished, return to the west side of the altar and face east. Say: "I invoke the rising of the Eternal Spiritual Sun! May I be illumined by its rays."

Then imagine before you, in the east, the first brilliant flash of the rising sun. As you watch, it slowly emerges from below the horizon, great and golden, its rays flooding the temple with light and life. Visualize the rising sun until it has cleared the horizon and appears whole before you. When this is done, raise your right hand, palm forward in salutation, and say, "In the presence of the holy powers of Nature, I proclaim this temple of the mysteries duly open." This completes the opening ritual.

At this point, if you are practicing the opening and closing ritual by themselves, go to the chair in the west, sit down, and enter into meditation for a short time. If you are performing one of the eight seasonal rituals of Merlin's Wheel, proceed to the ritual. Either way, when you are finished, return to the west of the altar, facing east, and begin the closing ritual, which is performed as follows:

First, purify the temple again with water, exactly the way you did in the opening.

Second, consecrate the temple with fire, exactly as in the opening.

Third, starting from west of the altar facing east, circumambulate the temple in the reverse direction, going counterclockwise, with the altar always to your left side. Do this so that you pass the east three times, then return to the altar. Standing again at the west side of the altar, facing east, say: "In the name of Hu the Mighty, Great Druid God, I set free any spirits who may have been imprisoned by this ceremony. Depart unto your rightful habitations in peace, and peace be between us."

This practice of formally releasing any spirits who may be imprisoned by a ceremony goes back centuries in Western occult practice. The traditional teaching behind this is that ritual workings produce a vortex of magical forces, and spiritual beings of various kinds can become caught in the vortex. Giving them "license to depart," as some old magical texts describe this, is common courtesy, and it also ensures that you won't have unwanted spiritual beings inhabiting your ritual space after the working is finished!

Fourth, perform the Lesser Banishing Ritual of the Pentagram, tracing the pentagrams counterclockwise from the uppermost point.

Fifth, standing at the west of the altar facing east, raise your right hand, palm facing the east, as you did in the opening. Say: "In the presence of the holy powers of Nature, I proclaim this temple closed." This completes the closing ritual.

For best results, this ritual should also be practiced until you can do it from memory, but it will take you a little more time to learn this than it took to learn the other rituals that have already been presented. If you don't have time to memorize the opening and closing ritual, take the time to rehearse it a few times, so that you don't have to fumble with it during the actual performance of the rituals. Even a little familiarity with the ritual will improve the results of the working considerably.

The Octagram

This is one of the distinctive symbolic patterns of the system of magic used in this book. At the Druid level, a complete ritual, the Ritual of the Octagram, uses this pattern to summon and banish the influences of the Tree of Life. At the Ovate and Bardic levels, the octagram is used by itself for this purpose, along with a spoken invocation.

As explained in chapter 3, the work of self-initiation calls on energies from seven of the spheres of the Tree of Life, plus an eighth point that sums up and focuses the energies of the three highest spheres. Since we work with these eight powers, the geometrical figure called the octagram—a star with eight points—allows us to symbolize those powers in visual terms, and to summon and banish them in ritual work. The Spheres of the Tree of Life are assigned to the octagram in the pattern shown below.

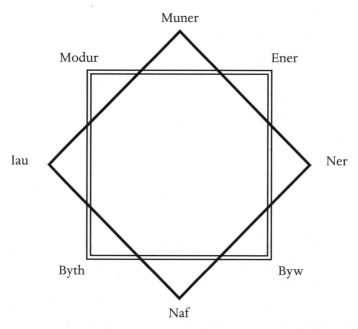

Figure 4–3: The Symbolic Octagram

In ritual work, on the other hand, a different version of the octagram is used, so that it can be traced in a single unbroken gesture. Using this version of the octagram, just as in the pentagram ritual, we trace clockwise from any given point to summon the powers associated with that point, and counter-clockwise to banish those powers.

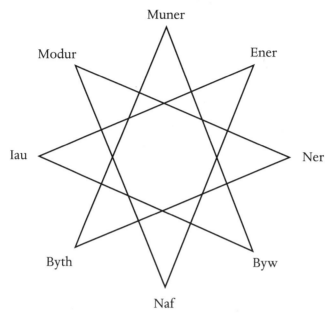

Figure 4–4: The Ritual Octagram

Symbolic Narrative

Each of the eight ceremonies of Merlin's Wheel has a narrative that is read aloud in the course of the ritual. If you compare these to the accounts of Merlin's life in the legends surveyed in chapter 2, you'll notice that no one legend includes all the details included in the symbolic narratives used here, or does so in exactly the same order. On the other hand, it's also true that no two of the legends of Merlin include all the details in the same order as any of the others!

The lesson to be learned here is that the legends of Merlin aren't sacred scriptures of the sort circulated by most of the mainstream religions of our society, and shouldn't be treated as such.[50] Like the varied stories about Demeter

---

50. A good case can be made, for that matter, that the stories about Jesus collected in the New Testament would reach more people and make more sense if they were treated as symbolically meaningful legends rather than turned into sacred scripture and believed in a rigidly literal way.

and Persephone that gave the mysteries of Eleusis, Agrai, and Andania their core narratives, the stories about Merlin take many shapes and have given rise to a wide range of different magical traditions and ritual celebrations. Neither the accounts of Geoffrey of Monmouth, nor the varied creations of medieval minstrels, nor these rituals can claim to offer "the one true story" about Merlin. Each narrative has its own lessons to teach and its own insights to communicate.

The symbolic narrative in each ritual of Merlin's Wheel should be read aloud, slowly and clearly, as though you were a wise elder reciting an ancient wisdom tale to a circle of young initiates. The reason it's important to read the narrative aloud is that this takes advantage of a little-known detail of the way the human nervous system works. When you read something aloud, it gets processed by the auditory centers on the sides of the brain, not just the thinking centers in the forebrain; it affects more of your brain and thus has stronger effects on your consciousness.[51] To the deeper levels of yourself, the experience of reading a narrative aloud has most of the same effects as hearing someone else read it, and this helps build the initiatory effect of the rituals.

Meditation

Many people these days think of meditation as something mysterious and exotic, but meditation has been part of magical training in the Western world since ancient times, and it plays a central role in the kind of initiatory magic taught in this book. The eight ritual workings of Merlin's Wheel each include a period of meditation in which the archetypal images and energies of the eight stations of the wheel settle into place in your consciousness. To make the most of that experience, you'll need to learn at least a little about meditation—and that means you'll need to work through some preliminary exercises, then practice meditation several times, before you begin the ritual work.

You may want to consider doing more than this. The regular practice of meditation is the most basic practice in most systems of magical initiation, and for good reason. It develops skills that make every other kind of magical work easier and more powerful, and also brings the kind of self-knowledge

---

51. This is why many people find that it's easier to memorize something if you read it aloud.

and self-awareness that keep the initiatory process on track. Ten or fifteen minutes a day of meditation will take you further, faster, than any other practice that exists. If daily practice is more than you can handle, one or two times a week will still bring good results. On the other hand, if this isn't the time for you to take on that form of magical training, you can still benefit from the meditation phase of each of the rituals.

For the preliminary exercises, you'll need a place that's quiet and not too brightly lit. It should be private—a room with a door you can shut is best, though if you can't arrange that, a quiet corner and a little forbearance on the part of your housemates will do the job. You'll need a chair with a straight back and a seat at a height that allows you to rest your feet flat on the floor while keeping your thighs level with the ground. You'll also need a clock or watch placed so that you can see it easily without moving your head.

The posture for Western meditation is much simpler, and more comfortable for most people, than the more famous postures used in Asian traditions. Sit on the chair with your feet and knees together or parallel, whichever is most comfortable for you. Your back should be straight but not stiff, your hands resting on your thighs, and your head rising as though a string fastened to the crown of your skull pulled it gently upward. Your eyes may be open or closed as you prefer; if they're open, they should look ahead of you but not focus on anything in particular. Practice the posture once or twice before starting work on the preliminary exercises.

The key to meditation is learning to enter a state of relaxed concentration. The word "relaxed" needs to be kept in mind here. Too often, what "concentration" suggests to modern people is a state of inner struggle: teeth clenched, eyes narrowed, the whole body taut with useless tension. This is the opposite of the state you need to reach. The exercises below will help you get to the state of calm and unstressed focus in which meditation happens.

Preliminary Exercise 1. Put yourself in the meditation position, then spend ten minutes or so just being aware of your physical body. Start at the soles of your feet and work your way slowly upward to the crown of your head. Take as much time as you wish. Notice any tensions you feel without trying to force yourself to relax; simply be aware of each tension. Over time this simple act of awareness will dissolve your body's habitual tensions by making them conscious and bringing up the rigid patterns of thought and emotion that form their foundations. Like so much in meditation, though, this process has to unfold at its own speed.

While you're doing this exercise, don't let yourself fidget and shift, no matter how much you want to. If your body starts itching, cramping, or reacting in some other way, simply be aware of the reaction, without responding to it. These reactions often become very intrusive during the early stages of meditation practice, but bear with them. They show you that you're getting past the levels of ordinary awareness. The discomforts you're feeling are actually there all the time; you've simply learned not to notice them. Once you let yourself perceive them again, you can relax into them and let them go.

Preliminary Exercise 2. Put several sessions into the first exercise until the posture begins to feel comfortable and balanced. At this point it's time to bring in the next ingredient of meditation, which is breathing. Start by sitting in your meditation position and going through the first exercise quickly, as a way of "checking in" with your physical body and settling into a comfortable and stable position. Then turn your attention to your breath. Draw in a deep breath and expel it slowly and steadily, until your lungs are completely empty.

When every last puff of air is out of your lungs, hold the breath out for a little while. Then breathe in through your nose, smoothly and evenly, until your lungs are full. Hold your breath in for a little while; it's important to hold the breath in by keeping the chest and belly expanded, not by shutting your throat, which can hurt your lungs.[52] Breathe out through your nose, smoothly and evenly. Each phase of the breath—breathing in, holding in, breathing out, holding out—should be approximately as long as the others, but you should let your body tell you how long to make each phase. This is called the Natural Breath, and while you're at this stage of learning you should continue doing it for ten minutes by the clock.

While you're breathing, your thoughts will likely try to go straying off toward some other topic. Don't let them. Keep your attention on the rhythm of the breathing, the feeling of the air moving through your nostrils and your lungs. Whenever you notice that you're thinking about something else, bring your attention gently back to your breathing. If your thoughts slip away

---

52. If you're not sure whether or not you're closing your throat while you hold your breath, try drawing in a little more breath if you're holding it in, and pushing out a little if you're holding it out. If your throat is closed, you'll feel it pop open.

again, bring them back again. This can be frustrating at first, but as with all things, it gets easier with practice.

Do the second preliminary exercise several times, until you're comfortable with it. At this point it's time to go on to actual meditation.

Practicing Meditation. The kind of meditation that's central to traditional methods of magical initiation differs from the sort of thing taught in most Asian mystical traditions in that it uses the thinking mind, rather than silencing it. To do this, you need a theme—that is, an idea or image you want to understand. Sit down in the meditation posture, and spend a minute or two going through the first preliminary exercise, being aware of your body and its tensions. Then begin the fourfold breath and continue it for five minutes by the clock. During these first steps, don't think about the theme, or for that matter, anything else. Simply be aware, first of your body and its tensions, then of your breathing, and allow your mind to become clear.

After five minutes, let your breathing become normal and turn your attention to the theme of the meditation. In each of the eight rituals, the theme will be the ritual itself, but while you're learning to meditate you'll need a more general theme, and the one I recommend for the purposes of this book is Merlin himself. Imagine him in one of the following eight forms—the wise infant in the arms of his mother; the child prophesying before King Vortigern; the boy standing amid the stones of Stonehenge; the young man receiving the infant Arthur from Ygerna's servants; the grown man at Arthur's coronation at Stonehenge; the man of middle years in the forest, beneath an apple tree; the old man at the seashore, standing beside Taliesin and Bedivere as the boat comes to carry the wounded Arthur away; or the wise elder seated outside his hermitage with his sister Ganieda, contemplating the heavens. Choose one of these, hold it in your mind, and see what ideas rise in your thoughts in response. Then choose one of these ideas and follow it out step by step, thinking about what it says to you, taking it as far as you can.

If you're meditating on Merlin as the wise infant, for example, imagine him in his mother's arms, looking out at the world with eyes that have far more than an infant's awareness in them. You don't have to visualize it, simply think about it, and pay attention to any ideas that rise in response. You might think of other mythological figures born of virgins who had unexpected knowledge from an early age—the biblical account of Jesus as a child going to the Temple and discussing scripture with the elderly scholars there, for example, has many parallels in legends from around the world. You might think of your own infancy, or of infants you have known; you might think about what infancy symbolizes, or speculate about why the wise child in mythology is always born around the winter solstice; or you might think of something else entirely. There are no wrong answers in meditation; the important thing is to pay attention to what your own mind has to teach you.

Unless you have quite a bit of experience in meditation, your thoughts will likely wander away from the theme again and again. Instead of simply bringing them back in a jump, follow them back through the chain of wandering thoughts until you reach the point where they left the theme. If you're meditating on Merlin the wise infant, for example, and suddenly notice that you're thinking about your grandmother instead, don't simply go back to Merlin and start again. Work your way back. What got you thinking about your grandmother? Memories of a Thanksgiving dinner when you were a child. What called up that memory? Recalling the taste of the roasted mixed nuts she used to put out for the guests. Where did that come from? Thinking about squirrels. Why squirrels? Because you heard the scuttling noise of a squirrel running across the roof above you, and it distracted you from thinking about Merlin.

Whenever your mind strays from the theme, bring it back up the track of wandering thoughts in this same way. This approach has two advantages. First of all, it has much to teach about the way your mind works, the flow of its thoughts, and the sort of associative leaps it likes to make. Second, it develops the habit of returning to the theme, and with practice you'll find that your thoughts will run back to the theme of your meditations just as enthusiastically as they run away from it. Time and regular practice will shorten the distance they run, until eventually your mind learns to run straight ahead along the meanings and implications of a theme without veering from it at all.

During your practice sessions, spend ten minutes meditating in this way and see what you learn about Merlin, and about yourself, in the process. As a good minimum, you may want to consider meditating eight times, once on each of the eight forms of Merlin, before your first ritual working. That should give you enough experience with the method that you can get something out of the practice even the first time you work one of the rituals of Merlin's Wheel.

†HE BARⱰic WORKⱠꞀCS

This second stage of the rituals of Merlin's Wheel builds on the foundations laid by the rituals of the Ovate Circle, bringing the power of creative imagination into the work. It also makes use of summonings and banishings of the four elements to heighten the magical dimension of the ritual. Each of the Bardic rituals includes the following steps:

1. Perform the opening ritual.
2. Perform one of the Elemental Summoning Rituals of the Pentagram.
3. Invoke the energies of the season with the Octagram and an invocation.
4. Perform the Composition of Place.
5. Read aloud the symbolic narrative of the season.
6. Meditate on the narrative and the energies of the season.
7. Dissolve the Composition of Place.
8. Release the energies of the season with the Octagram and words of thanks.
9. Perform one of the Elemental Banishing Rituals of the Pentagram.
10. Perform the closing ritual.

The basic framework is the same, as already mentioned, but two additional stages are added at the beginning and end of each ritual. The Elemental Rituals of the Pentagram are used to summon and banish the forces of the individual elements and will need to be learned and practiced before you use them in ritual. The Composition of Place is simply a matter of reading a description of a scene and imagining that scene as vividly as you can, and can be done by most people without advance practice. A clear understanding of the theory and purpose of both these parts of the ritual, however, will make both of them more effective when you use them.

The Elemental Rituals of the Pentagram

There are four Elemental Rituals of the Pentagram, one for each of the four traditional elements of earth, water, air, and fire. They follow the same structure as the Lesser Ritual, but trace the pentagrams differently, call on different divine names, and use different words when calling on the powers of the four quarters.

The Ritual of the Earth Pentagram. This is performed with one of the two pentagrams of earth, as shown below—the first to summon, and the second to banish. Begin with the Rite of the Rays, as in the Lesser Ritual, then go to the east and trace the earth pentagram. Point at the center and vibrate the divine name CERNUNNOS (pronounced "ker-NOON-os"). Proceed as in the Lesser Ritual to the other four quarters, drawing a line of light as you go, tracing the same pentagram and vibrating the same name in each. When you have completed the circle and return to the altar, say: "Before me the fertile plains, behind me the rolling hills, to my right hand the tall mountains, to my left hand the deep caverns, for about me stand the pentagrams and upon me shine the Three Rays of Light." Then end with the Rite of the Rays as usual.

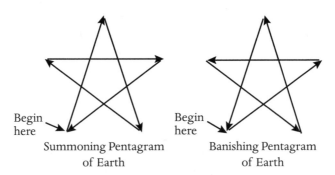

Summoning Pentagram
of Earth

Banishing Pentagram
of Earth

Figure 4–5: Pentagrams of Earth

The Ritual of the Water Pentagram. This is performed with one or the other of the two pentagrams of water, as shown below—the first to summon, the second to banish. Begin with the Rite of the Rays, as in the Lesser Ritual, and go to the east and trace the water pentagram. Point at the center and vibrate the divine name SIRONA (pronounced "si-ROE-na"). Proceed as in the Lesser Ritual to the other four quarters, drawing a line of light as you go, tracing the same pentagram and vibrating the same name in each. When you have completed the circle and return to the altar, say: "Before me the dancing streams, behind me the great ocean, to my right hand the strong rivers, to my left hand the quiet lakes, for about me stand the pentagrams and upon me shine the Three Rays of Light." Then end with the Rite of the Rays as usual.

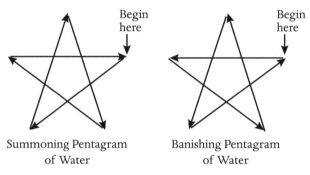

Summoning Pentagram   Banishing Pentagram
of Water   of Water

Figure 4–6: Pentagrams of Water

The Ritual of the Air Pentagram. This is performed with one or the other of the two pentagrams of air, as shown on the next page—the first to invoke, and the second to banish. Begin with the Rite of the Rays, as in the Lesser Ritual, and go to the east and trace the air pentagram. Point at the center and vibrate the divine name BELISAMA (pronounced "BEL-ih-SAH-ma"). Proceed as in the Lesser Ritual to the other four quarters, drawing a line of light as you go, tracing the same pentagram and vibrating the same name in each. When you have completed the circle and return to the altar, say: "Before me the rushing wind, behind me the silver mist, to my right hand the shining sky, to my left hand the billowing cloud, for about me stand the pentagrams and upon me shine the Three Rays of Light." Then end with the Rite of the Rays as usual.

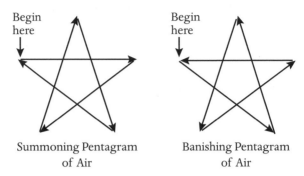

Figure 4–7: Pentagrams of Air

The Ritual of the Fire Pentagram. This is performed with one or the other of the two pentagrams of fire, as shown below—the first to invoke, and the second to banish. Begin with the Rite of the Rays, as in the Lesser Ritual, and go to the east and trace the fire pentagram. Point at the center and vibrate the divine name TOUTATIS (pronounced "too-TAUGHT-is"). Proceed as in the Lesser Ritual to the other four quarters, drawing a line of light as you go, tracing the same pentagram and vibrating the same name in each. When you have completed the circle and return to the altar, say: "Before me the lightning flash, behind me the fire of growth, to my right hand the radiant sun, to my left hand the flame upon the hearth, for about me stand the pentagrams and upon me shine the Three Rays of Light." Then end with the Rite of the Rays as usual.

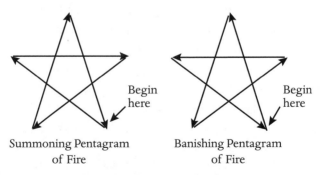

Figure 4–8: Pentagrams of Fire

These rituals, as already noted, need to be learned and practiced before you use them in one of the seasonal ceremonies. Having them committed to memory is best, but it's enough at first to have done each of them several times so that you can do them with only a glance at a "cheat sheet" giving the pentagrams, names, and words.

The Composition of Place

The human imagination is one of the great tools of magic, and ceremonial magic uses it in a galaxy of ways. The practice of Composition of Place is one of these. It's simply a matter of building up an imagined location as vividly as possible so that the symbolic qualities of that location will pervade the space in which the working takes place.

Those words, "as vividly as possible," can be taken more strongly than they should. So many of us have been exposed to so much visual media—television, movies, video games—that many people tend to think that this sort of photographic, hyperrealistic imagery is the only kind that matters. Not many people can achieve that level of mental imagery even with extensive training, and very, very few can do anything of the kind the first time they try. If you're not one of those few, don't worry about it. The kind of imagery you experience in your daydreams and your memories is quite vivid enough for our purposes.

It may be helpful to remember that these images are meant to be taken symbolically, not literally. Like the symbolic narratives introduced in the Ovate Circle, they are meant to involve the deeper levels of your mind, not just the surface layers of ordinary thinking. Dragons don't exist in our world, but they are still powerful symbols; in exactly the same way, the image of a barefoot woman in a cold winter scene (for example) may not be historically accurate but it communicates certain symbolic meanings far more precisely and powerfully than any mere rehash of historical details can do. The question to ask yourself in meditation, as you consider the images you've built up in the Composition of Place, is not "did this actually happen?" but "what does this mean?" As the famous British mage Dion Fortune wrote about a different set of magical pictures, "these images are not descriptive but symbolic, and are designed to train the mind, not to inform it."[53]

It's a good idea, before you use the Composition of Place in a ritual, to read through the description at least twice and get a general sense of the image you're going to build up. Once you've done that, start from the beginning of the description and imagine each detail in the order in which they're described. Once you've finished, spend a few moments seeing the entire image as a whole as clearly as you can.

You'll almost certainly find that the first time you imagine each of the images in Merlin's Wheel, you'll be able to perceive only a vague sketch of the image described in the ritual. Here as elsewhere, though, practice makes perfect—and something more than mere practice is involved. Each time you perform the Composition of Place with a specific image, that image becomes easier to call back to mind later because you're literally building it on the subtle planes of being with your imaginative efforts. As you continue working with the rituals of Merlin's Wheel, year after year, the Composition of Place will become more and more vivid and charged with emotion until it forms a powerful element of the whole rite.

As each ritual winds up, finally, you'll be asked to dissolve the Composition of Place. This is much easier than the Composition of Place itself; you simply picture the image you've created dissolving and going away, so that its influence doesn't stray from your magical work into the details of everyday life. If you think of the building up of the Composition of Place as being like fiddling with the dial of an old-fashioned radio to get the station you want, and the dissolving of the Composition of Place as giving the dial a good twist to make sure the radio won't keep on playing that station, you'll understand the gist of what's going on.

†HE DRᵱID WORKᵯGS

These are the complete forms of the rituals of Merlin's Wheel, and they expand on the framework already developed to provide an initiatory experience that can be repeated year after year with good results. Each of the Druid rituals includes the following steps:

---

53. Fortune, *The Cosmic Doctrine*, 11.

1. Perform the opening ritual.

2. Perform one of the Summoning Rituals of the Octagram.

3. Perform the Composition of Place.

4. Read aloud the symbolic narrative of the season.

5. Call down the energies of the season into the communion mead, and drink it.

6. Meditate on the narrative and the energies of the season.

7. Dissolve the Composition of Place.

8. Release the energies of the season with words of thanks.

9. Perform one of the Banishing Rituals of the Octagram.

10. Perform the closing ritual.

The ceremonies of the Druid level involve two changes from the Bardic level. First, the elemental pentagram rituals are replaced by the rituals of the octagram, which call on the influences of the Tree of Life directly. Second, a communion ceremony is used to bring those influences into the physical body of the practitioner by charging a cup of mead (or honey water, for those who don't feel it appropriate to use alcohol) with the energies of the season using ritual methods, offering some to the deity who governs that seasonal festival, and drinking the rest. The act of taking consecrated food or drink into the body of the participant was a common feature of mystery initiations in ancient times, and it plays an important part in the workings of Merlin's Wheel once the necessary skill with ritual has been attained.

The Octagram Rituals

There are sixteen octagram rituals, one to summon and one to banish for each of the eight points of the octagram and the eight energies of the Tree of Life they command. As with the elemental pentagram rituals, the differences between one and another octagram ritual are simply which point you choose to start tracing the octagram, which direction you trace it, which color of light you visualize as you trace the line, and which divine name you vibrate while pointing to the center.

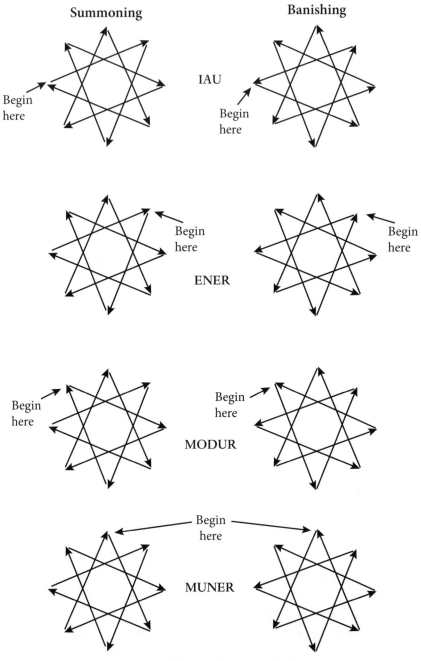

Figures 4–9a and 4–9b: Octagrams

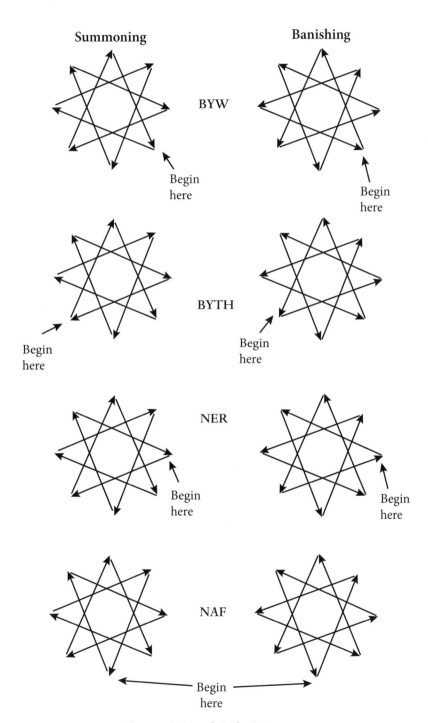

Figures 4–9a and 4–9b: Octagrams

Sphere of the Tree	Color
Iau	White
Ener	Blue
Modur	Red
Muner	Yellow
Byw	Green
Byth	Orange
Ner	Violet
Naf	Indigo

Table 4–2: Colors for the Ritual of the Octagram

In the octagram rituals, the Rite of the Rays and the tracing of an octa-gram in each of the four quarters is combined with a ritual called the In-vocation of Celi. In the traditions of the Druid Revival, Celi is the Hidden One, the mysterious divine source from which all things flow, who appears in certain legends as an unseen presence piping on the hills, and in certain others as the secret fire of blessing and magic. In the rite, three gestures are used to invoke the three aspects of Celi. A great deal of Druidical teaching is concealed in these three signs, and they and their titles make good themes for meditation.

The Ritual of the Octagram is performed as follows:

First, perform the Rite of the Rays, just as in the Pentagram ritual.

Second, go to the eastern quarter of the space and trace the appropriate octagram to summon or banish, beginning from the point corresponding to the Sphere whose influence you want to work with, and tracing clockwise to invoke and counterclockwise to banish. As you trace the octagram, visualize your fingers drawing a line of light in the color corresponding to the Sphere, as shown in table 4–2.

Third, trace a line of the same color with fingers or wand around to the southern quarter of the space and repeat the process, tracing the same octa-gram as before. Then do the same to the west and north, and finally return to the east, having traced the same octagram in each quarter and also traced a circle entirely around the place of working, as you do when you perform a pentagram ritual.

Fourth, return to the center and perform the Invocation of Celi. This is done with the following words and actions:

Make the Sign of the Bounty of Nature, as follows. Extend your left hand down and out to your side in a straight line, hand extended, palm facing forward. Place your right hand, palm up, at the level of your solar plexus, so that your forearm is parallel to the ground; your elbow is extended out to your side. Say aloud: "The Bounty of Nature."

Figure 4–10: Sign of the Bounty of Nature

Make the Sign of the Cauldron of Annwn, as follows. Raise both arms to the sides, curving them to form the outline of a cauldron; the hands are a little above head level, with the fingertips pointing straight up and the palms facing each other. Say aloud: "The Cauldron of Annwn." (This word is pronounced "ANN-oon.")

Figure 4–11: Sign of the Cauldron of Annwn

Make the Sign of the Child of Light, as follows. Bring the fingertips of your right hand to the point of your left shoulder; allow your right forearm to rest across your chest in a diagonal line so that your right elbow is at your right side; bring your left hand across so that the fingers cup the right elbow, the left forearm being parallel to the ground and the left elbow being at the left side. Say aloud: "The Child of Light."

Figure 4–12: Sign of the Child of Light

Sweep your hands out and down, straightening your arms and holding them out from your body at an angle so that your arms and body form the sign of the Three Rays of Light. Say: "All are one in the infinite CELI." (The name Celi is vibrated, and pronounced "KEH-lee.")

Fifth, perform the Rite of the Rays again to finish the ritual.

✧

Like the Pentagram Rituals, the Octagram Ritual should be practiced several times before you try to use it in a ceremony. Committing it to memory is best, but if this is difficult, it's sufficient to become familiar enough with the ritual that you can do it smoothly with a glance at a "cheat sheet" to remind you of the right point of the octagram to begin with and the right color to use for the line you trace. The tracing of the octagram itself may require a little practice, as it's a somewhat complex figure. Take the time you need to learn how to trace it, and the resulting ritual work will be better for it.

The Consecration of the Mead

For each of the ceremonies of the Druid Grade, you will need a cup, chalice, or horn containing mead, which is placed on the altar. A drinking horn has long been traditional for this purpose in the Druid Revival, but not everyone can obtain one of these; a ritual chalice or, if that isn't an option for you, an ordinary wine glass will be sufficient.

Mead is available at many American liquor stores these days, and it's also the easiest of alcoholic beverages to brew yourself.[54] If you are underage, or for some other reason either should not or do not wish to use an alcoholic beverage in ritual, you can make a workable substitute by mixing a teaspoonful of honey into a cup of hot water. Stir thoroughly until the honey is dissolved, then let the mixture cool to room temperature.

You will need enough mead (or honey water) to pour out an offering, and still have as much left as you wish to drink. If you can perform the ritual outside, the mead can be poured directly on the ground. If not, you will need a wide bowl large enough to receive the offering, which can be set on the floor or on any convenient flat surface near the altar. After the ritual, the mead in the bowl should be taken outside and poured on the ground, or into running water.

The horn, chalice, or glass of mead goes onto the altar before the ritual begins, and remains there until the fifth step of the ritual. At this point you recite the invocation, calling on the deity who presides over that station of Merlin's Wheel to be present and bless you, then perform a ritual called the Analysis of OIW.

---

54. *The Compleat Meadmaker* by Ken Schramm is a good introduction to the art of making mead in small batches at home.

The word OIW is a cryptogram. In the traditions of the Druid Revival, it is used in place of a certain very secret name or word of power, which is called the Secret of the Bards of the Island of Britain. This ritual discloses one part of its meaning, by way of a myth of origins found in old Welsh Druid writings. Here is one version of the story:

> Einigan the Giant beheld three pillars of light, having in them all demonstrable sciences that ever were, or ever will be. And he took three rods of the quicken tree, and placed on them the forms and signs of all sciences, so as to be remembered; and exhibited them. But those who saw them misunderstood, and falsely apprehended them, and taught illusive sciences, regarding the rods as a God, whereas they only bore His Name. When Einigan saw this he was greatly annoyed, and in the intensity of his grief he broke the three rods, nor were others found that contained accurate sciences. He was so distressed on this account that from the intensity he burst asunder, and with his parting breath he prayed God that there should be accurate sciences among men in the flesh, and there should be a correct understanding for the proper discernment thereof. And at the end of a year and a day after the decease of Einigan, Menw, son of the Three Shouts, beheld three rods growing out of the mouth of Einigan, which exhibited the sciences of the Ten Letters, and the mode in which the sciences of language and speech were arranged by them, and in language and speech all distinguishable sciences. He then took the rods, and taught from them the sciences—all, except the Name of God, which he made a secret, lest the Name should be falsely discerned; and hence arose the Secret of the Bards of the Island of Britain.[55]

Einigan the Giant, Einigan Gawr in Welsh, is the Adam of the Druid Revival traditions, the first of all created beings. (His name is pronounced "EYE-ne-gan," with the "g" hard as in "get" rather than soft as in "gel." In ancient Celtic times this name was Oinogenos, "the one born alone"—another divine title like those we surveyed in chapter 2.) The three pillars or rays

---

55. Williams ab Ithel, *The Barddas of Iolo Morganwg*, 49–51.

of light he beheld were the rays of divine power that created the world and spelled out the secret name of Celi the Hidden One. Each ray has a name, and these are the same three names you recite in the Rite of the Rays: Gwron, the Knowledge of Awen, is the left hand ray; Plennydd, the Power of Awen, is the right hand ray; and Alawn, the Peace of Awen, is the central ray.

The Analysis of OIW is performed as follows:

Stand at the west of the altar, facing east, and say aloud, "In the beginning of things, Einigen Gawr, the first of all created beings, beheld three rays of light descending from the heavens, in which were all the knowledge that ever was and ever will be. These same were three voices and the three letters of one name, the Name of the Infinite One. Gwron, Plennydd, and Alawn; Knowledge, Power, and Peace.

"A, Knowledge, the sign of the Bounty of Nature." Make the Sign of the Bounty of Nature, just as you did in the octagram ritual.

"W, Power, the sign of the Cauldron of Annwn." Make the Sign of the Cauldron of Annwn.

"N, Peace, the sign of the Child of Light." Make the third Sign, the Sign of the Child of Light.

"A." Make the Sign of the Bounty of Nature again. "W." Make the Sign of the Cauldron of Annwn again. "N." Make the Sign of the Child of Light again. "AWEN." (Pronounce this "AH-OO-EN," drawing out the syllables, and making the three Signs again, one with each syllable.) Then lower your arms and continue: "As in that hour, so in this, may the light that was before the worlds descend!" Visualize a ray of light descending from infinite space above you into the cup or horn of mead, transforming the mead into pure light.

Hold that image as long and as intensely as you can. When your concentration begins to waver, release the image and lift up the cup or horn of mead in both hands. Say: "[*Name of deity*], receive this offering as I receive your blessing." Pour out some of the mead onto the ground or into the offering bowl. Then raise the cup or horn again and drink the remainder, concentrating on the idea that the energies you have invoked in the ritual are entering your body with the mead to become part of you.

✧

The rituals and other practices covered in this chapter are the tools you'll need to enact the mysteries of Merlin's Wheel. Once you've learned the elements of the Ovate workings and practiced them enough to do them fairly smoothly, you're ready to begin. In the chapters ahead, we'll walk through the eight rituals of Merlin's Wheel in each of the three circles, and show how the ritual elements come together to help attune your consciousness with the deep spiritual realities woven into the tale of the god Moridunos-Maponos, Merlin the Mabon—a tale that never happened, but always *is*.

—— CHAPTER FIVE ——

THE OVATE CIRCLE

The Ovate Circle is the first and most basic level of work in the mysteries of Merlin. It uses the least complex and demanding ceremonies, so it can be done by anyone, no matter how inexperienced, who is willing to invest a little time in studying and practicing the rituals and other practices covered in chapter 4 of this book. Its effects are correspondingly subtle, and those who expect vast revelations or an instant expansion of magical or spiritual power, beyond what regular practice and training will produce, will be disappointed. Those who pay close attention, though, will discover that the practice of these rituals will build foundations far more sturdy than those of Vortigern's legendary tower.

While it's best to begin the sequence of rituals with the ceremony of Alban Arthan, the winter solstice, not everyone will have that opportunity, nor is it required of you to wait until winter comes around again. You can begin the rituals at any point in the seasonal cycle. The one requirement is that you need to complete the entire sequence of Ovate rituals at least once in order to avoid the unbalancing effect that a partial performance of the cycle would produce. Plan on spending a full year at this level before you proceed to the rituals of the Bardic Circle.

──── ALBAⁿ ARTHAⁿ, DECEMBER 21 ────

Before starting, set up your working space as a temple. The altar is at the center with a brown altar cloth. On it are three white candles in candlesticks, a bowl or cauldron of water, and a bowl or cauldron of sand on which to burn incense; you may also, if you wish, put on the altar any seasonal decorations suitable to the place where you live. Place a chair in the west facing the altar. Sit there for a few moments of silence to calm your mind and focus on the ritual work you are about to do, then stand up, go to the altar, and begin.

First, perform the complete opening ritual as given in chapter 4.

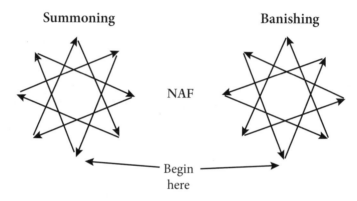

Figure 5–1: Octagrams of Naf

Second, standing at the west of the altar facing east, trace the summoning Octagram of Naf in the air above the altar, as shown in figure 5–1, using the first two fingers of your right hand. Imagine your fingers drawing the octagram in a line of indigo light. Then point to the center of the octagram and say the following, vibrating the name written in capital letters:

In the sacred name OLWEN and by the holy hawthorn, I call upon the powers of Naf the Shaper, the Tenth Sphere of the Tree of Life, to hallow and bless this ritual of Alban Arthan, and awaken for me the first station of Merlin's Wheel. Olwen of the White Track, maiden goddess of the Tenth Sphere, I pray that you will bless and guide me in this work of self-initiation.

Third, bow or curtsy to the divine presence you have invoked, and take your seat in the west. Read aloud the narrative of the season in a clear, slow voice:

The king asked her, "Who is the father of your child?" And the princess answered, "I know not. All I know is that when I dwelt in my father's house with my maidens, one night while I slept, there appeared to me one in the form of a handsome young man who spoke to me and kissed me, then vanished so that I could no longer see him. Often thereafter he came to me, sometimes visibly and sometimes not, and at length he lay beside me and made love to me as a man would, and after that I found that I was with child. Now you must decide what this child's father was, for apart from that, I have never been with a man."

And the king sent for Magan the wise, his counselor, and when Magan had heard the whole story he said, "In the books of the sages it is written that many a child has been born in this way. For there are a race of spirits who dwell between the earth and the moon who are partly of the nature of men and partly of the nature of angels, and when they wish they can assume mortal form and cohabit with human beings. It is possible that one of these appeared to this woman and begot the child upon her."

Fourth, meditate for a time on the narrative. Five or ten minutes of meditation should be a workable minimum at the Ovate stage of the work.

Fifth, rise from the chair and go to the west of the altar facing east. Standing there, trace the banishing Octagram of Naf in the air above the altar, as shown in figure 5–1, using the first two fingers of your right hand. Imagine your fingers drawing the octagram in a line of indigo light. Then point to the center of the octagram and say the following, vibrating the name written in capital letters:

In the sacred name OLWEN and by the holy hawthorn, I thank the powers of Naf the Shaper, the Tenth Sphere of the Tree of Life, for hallowing and blessing this ritual of Alban Arthan, and awakening for me the first station of Merlin's Wheel. Olwen of the White Track, maiden goddess of the Tenth Sphere, I thank you for your help in this work of self-initiation.

Sixth, bow or curtsy to the divine presence and then perform the complete closing ritual as given in chapter 4.

———— CALAN MYRI, FEBRUARY 2 ————

Before starting, set up your working space as a temple. The altar is at the center with a violet altar cloth. On it are three white candles in candlesticks, a bowl or cauldron of water, and a bowl or cauldron of sand on which to burn incense; you may also, if you wish, put on the altar any seasonal decorations suitable to the place where you live. Place a chair in the west facing the altar. Sit there for a few moments of silence to calm your mind and focus on the ritual work you are about to do, then stand up, go to the altar, and begin.

First, perform the complete opening ritual as given in chapter 4.

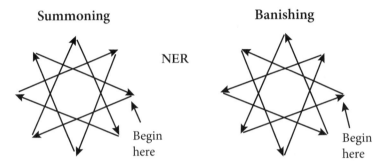

Figure 5–2: Octagrams of Ner

Second, standing at the west of the altar facing east, trace the summoning Octagram of Ner, as shown in figure 5–2, in the air above the altar using the first two fingers of your right hand. Imagine your fingers drawing the octagram in a line of violet light. Then point to the center of the octagram and say the following. The name that you vibrate should be the one of the opposite gender to that of your physical body to establish a polarity between you and the deity[56]—thus men should vibrate the name Sul (pronounced "SEEL"), while women vibrate the name Coel (pronounced "CO-ell").[57]

> In the sacred name (SUL or COEL) and by the holy willow, I call upon the powers of Ner the Mighty, the Ninth Sphere of the Tree of Life, to hallow and bless this ritual of Calan Myri and awaken for me the second station of Merlin's Wheel. Sul of the healing Springs (or) Coel the master of the wild places, goddess (or) god of the Ninth Sphere, I pray that you will bless and guide me in this work of self-initiation.

Third, bow or curtsy to the divine presence you have invoked and take your seat in the west. Read aloud the narrative of the season in a clear, slow voice:

> Then the boy spoke to King Vortigern, saying, "Your wise men have lied to you, for they do not know what lies beneath this hill. Command your servants to dig and they will find a pool hidden beneath the ground. Let them dig channels and drain away the water and then a marvel will be seen. For beneath the water lie two hollow stones, and under the stones lie two great dragons, and it is they who will not permit your tower to stand."
>
> So the king commanded his servants to dig, and soon they discovered the pool and marveled at the boy's wisdom. They dug channels and drained away the water and found the two hollow stones. Then the king sat beside the empty pool and watched, and the two dragons came forth from the hollow stones. One of them was white and

---

56. In magical philosophy, each person is alternately male and female on different planes of being, which is why the physical body is the important marker here. (For other kinds of magical work, the gender of other aspects of your being is more important.) If you happen to be intersex or transgender, you may need to experiment to determine which gender of deity will polarize properly with you at this station. The wrong choice will produce a sense of energy blockage or "stuckness." Fortunately this blockage will go away promptly without causing harm, unless the wrong invocation is repeated many times.

57. Students of *The Celtic Golden Dawn* will notice that this differs from the Exercise of the Central Ray, in which you vibrate the name that corresponds to your body's physical gender. Different workings require different names.

the other red, and they leapt upon each other, biting and clawing and breathing fire, so that no struggle so fierce had ever been seen in that land. Then the king turned to the boy and asked him what the combat between the dragons meant. At once Merlin burst into tears and began to prophesy.

Fourth, meditate for a time on the narrative. Five or ten minutes of meditation should be a workable minimum at the Ovate stage of the work.

Fifth, rise from the chair and go to the west of the altar facing east. Standing there, trace the banishing Octagram of Ner, as shown in figure 5–2, in the air above the altar using the first two fingers of your right hand. Imagine your fingers drawing the octagram in a line of indigo light. Then point to the center of the octagram and say the following, vibrating the name written in capital letters:

In the sacred name (SUL or COEL) and by the holy willow, I thank the powers of Ner the Mighty, the Ninth Sphere of the Tree of Life, for hallowing and blessing this ritual of Calan Myri, and awakening for me the second station of Merlin's Wheel. Sul of the healing springs (or) Coel the master of the wild places, goddess (or) god of the Ninth Sphere, I thank you for your help in this work of self-initiation.

Sixth, bow or curtsy to the divine presence and then perform the complete closing ritual as given in chapter 4.

——— ALBAN EILIR, MARCH 21 ———

Before starting, set up your working space as a temple. The altar is at the center with an orange altar cloth. On it are three white candles in candlesticks, a bowl or cauldron of water, and a bowl or cauldron of sand on which to burn incense; you may also, if you wish, put on the altar any seasonal decorations suitable to the place where you live. Place a chair in the west facing the altar. Sit there for a few moments of silence to calm your mind and focus on the ritual work you are about to do, then stand up, go to the altar, and begin.

First, perform the complete opening ritual as given in chapter 4.

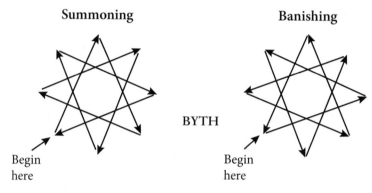

Figure 5–3: Octagrams of Byth

Second, standing at the west of the altar facing east, trace the summoning Octagram of Byth, as shown in figure 5–3, in the air above the altar using the first two fingers of your right hand. Imagine your fingers drawing the octagram in a line of orange light. Then point to the center of the octagram and say the following, vibrating the name written in capital letters:

In the sacred name MABON and by the holy hazel, I call upon the powers of Byth the Eternal, the Eighth Sphere of the Tree of Life, to hallow and bless this ritual of Alban Eilir, and awaken for me the third station of Merlin's Wheel. Mabon, son of Modron, ever-young god of the Eighth Sphere, I pray that you will bless and guide me in this work of self-initiation.

Third, bow or curtsy to the divine presence you have invoked, and take your seat in the west. Read aloud the narrative of the season in a clear, slow voice:

> And Merlin said to Aurelius, "If you wish a fitting monument, let the stones of the Giants' Dance in the uttermost west be brought here and set in a ring. For those stones were brought from distant places and hallowed by secret rites in the most ancient times, and each one has healing powers." This counsel seemed good to Aurelius, and he sent his brother Uther and a great host of men and Merlin to bring back the stones of the Giants' Dance.
>
> And when they had driven off the guardians of the stones, Uther and his men tried to draw the stones from the earth to bear them back to Britain, but they could not make a single stone yield to all their efforts. Then Merlin laughed, set out such gear as he required, and easily drew up the stones and conveyed them to the ships, and they brought the stones back to the plain of Salisbury with great rejoicing. There, by Merlin's art, the great stones were set up in a mighty ring, and there the people of Britain made festival, and there Aurelius was crowned King of the Britons.

Fourth, meditate for a time on the narrative. Five or ten minutes of meditation should be a workable minimum at the Ovate stage of the work.

Fifth, rise from the chair and go to the west of the altar facing east. Standing there, trace the banishing Octagram of Byth, as shown in figure 5–3, in the air above the altar, using the first two fingers of your right hand. Imagine your fingers drawing the octagram in a line of orange light. Then point to the center of the octagram and say the following, vibrating the name written in capital letters:

> In the sacred name MABON and by the holy hazel, I thank the powers of Byth the Eternal, the Eighth Sphere of the Tree of Life, for hallowing and blessing this ritual of Alban Eilir, and awakening for me the

third station of Merlin's Wheel. Mabon, son of Modron, ever-young god of the Eighth Sphere, I thank you for your help in this work of self-initiation.

Sixth, bow or curtsy to the divine presence and then perform the complete closing ritual as given in chapter 4.

—— CALAN MAI, MAY I ——

Before starting, set up your working space as a temple. The altar is at the center with a green altar cloth. On it are three white candles in candlesticks, a bowl or cauldron of water, and a bowl or cauldron of sand on which to burn incense; you may also, if you wish, put on the altar any seasonal decorations suitable to the place where you live. Place a chair in the west facing the altar. Sit there for a few moments of silence to calm your mind and focus on the ritual work you are about to do, then stand up, go to the altar, and begin.

First, perform the complete opening ritual as given in chapter 4.

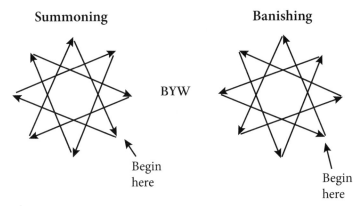

Figure 5–4: Octagrams of Byw

Second, standing at the west of the altar facing east, trace the summoning Octagram of Byw, as shown in figure 5–4, in the air above the altar using the first two fingers of your right hand. Imagine your fingers drawing the octagram in a line of emerald-green light. Then point to the center of the octagram and say the following, vibrating the name written in capital letters:

In the sacred name ELEN and by the holy apple tree, I call upon the powers of Byw the Living, the Seventh Sphere of the Tree of Life, to hallow and bless this ritual of Calan Mai, and awaken for me the fourth station of Merlin's Wheel. Elen of the roads and the twilight, goddess of the Seventh Sphere, I pray that you will bless and guide me in this work of self-initiation.

Third, bow or curtsy to the divine presence you have invoked, and take your seat in the west. Read aloud the narrative of the season in a clear, slow voice:

And King Uther said to Merlin, "Give me one night of love with the lady Ygerna, and in return I will give you whatever you will ask." And Merlin replied to him, "So be it." And he changed Uther's appearance to that of Ygerna's husband the Duke of Cornwall. That night Uther rode to the castle of Tintagel and Ygerna received him lovingly, thinking he was her husband. That night was Arthur the Pendragon conceived, and that same night the Duke of Cornwall died.

When nine months had passed and Ygerna gave birth to an infant boy, Merlin went to Uther and said, "When I brought you to Ygerna you promised me whatever I would ask. I ask now for the child you begot upon her." And the king commanded the nursemaid to take the infant to Merlin, who waited beside the sea. And he took Arthur to a hidden place where he was fostered with a worthy family and did not know his birth or his heritage.

Fourth, meditate for a time on the narrative. Five or ten minutes of meditation should be a workable minimum at the Ovate stage of the work.

Fifth, rise from the chair and go to the west of the altar facing east. Standing there, trace the banishing Octagram of Byw, as shown in figure 5–4, in the air above the altar using the first two fingers of your right hand. Imagine your fingers drawing the octagram in a line of emerald-green light. Then point to the center of the octagram and say the following, vibrating the name written in capital letters:

In the sacred name ELEN and by the holy apple, I thank the powers of Byw the Living, the Seventh Sphere of the Tree of Life, for hallowing and blessing this ritual of Calan Mai, and awakening for me the fourth station of Merlin's Wheel. Elen of the roads and the twilight, maiden goddess of the Tenth Sphere, I thank you for your help in this work of self-initiation.

Sixth, bow or curtsy to the divine presence and then perform the complete closing ritual as given in chapter 4.

──── ALBAN HEFIN, JUNE 21 ────

Before starting, set up your working space as a temple. The altar is at the center with a gold altar cloth. On it are three white candles in candlesticks, a bowl or cauldron of water, and a bowl or cauldron of sand on which to burn incense; you may also, if you wish, put on the altar any seasonal decorations suitable to the place where you live. Place a chair in the west facing the altar. Sit there for a few moments of silence to calm your mind and focus on the ritual work you are about to do, then stand up, go to the altar, and begin.

First, perform the complete opening ritual as given in chapter 4.

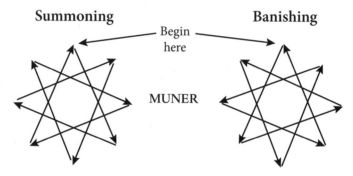

Figure 5–5: Octagrams of Muner

Second, standing at the west of the altar facing east, trace the summoning Octagram of Muner, as shown in figure 5–5, in the air above the altar using the first two fingers of your right hand. Imagine your fingers drawing the octagram in a line of golden light. Then point to the center of the octagram and say the following, vibrating the name written in capital letters:

In the sacred name ESUS and by the holy oak, I call upon the powers of Muner the Lord, the Sixth Sphere of the Tree of Life, to hallow and bless this ritual of Alban Hefin, and awaken for me the fifth station of Merlin's Wheel. Esus, chief of tree-spirits, god of the Sixth Sphere, I pray that you will bless and guide me in this work of self-initiation.

Third, bow or curtsy to the divine presence you have invoked, and take your seat in the west. Read aloud the narrative of the season in a clear, slow voice:

Then Arthur once more lightly drew the sword out of the stone. But the barons said, "Who is this youth that he should reign over us?" And Merlin answered them, "This is Arthur, who is the son of Uther Pendragon. By right of blood, as also by right of drawing the sword from the stone as you have seen this day, he is to be King of the Britons." This the barons would not allow. But when word went forth that the barons still refused their homage to Arthur, the common people of the country rose up as one and said, "We will have Arthur as our king, and he who would deny him the crown, him we will slay."

So the barons knelt before Arthur and did him homage, and Merlin anointed him and placed the crown that had been his father's upon his head. And so did Arthur become King of the Britons, and long held the realm of Logres in peace.

Fourth, meditate for a time on the narrative. Five or ten minutes of meditation should be a workable minimum at the Ovate stage of the work.

Fifth, rise from the chair and go to the west of the altar facing east. Standing there, trace the banishing Octagram of Muner, as shown in figure 5–5, in the air above the altar using the first two fingers of your right hand. Imagine your fingers drawing the octagram in a line of golden light. Then point to the center of the octagram and say the following, vibrating the name written in capital letters:

In the sacred name ESUS and by the holy oak, I thank the powers of Muner the Lord, the Sixth Sphere of the Tree of Life, for hallowing and blessing this ritual of Alban Hefin, and awakening for me the fifth station of Merlin's Wheel. Esus, chief of tree-spirits, god of the Sixth Sphere, I thank you for your help in this work of self-initiation.

Sixth, bow or curtsy to the divine presence and then perform the complete closing ritual as given in chapter 4.

─────── CALAN GWYNGALAF, AUGUST I ───────

Before starting, set up your working space as a temple. The altar is at the center with a red altar cloth. On it are three white candles in candlesticks, a bowl or cauldron of water, and a bowl or cauldron of sand on which to burn incense; you may also, if you wish, put on the altar any seasonal decorations suitable to the place where you live. Place a chair in the west facing the altar. Sit there for a few moments of silence to calm your mind and focus on the ritual work you are about to do, then stand up, go to the altar, and begin.

First, perform the complete opening ritual as given in chapter 4.

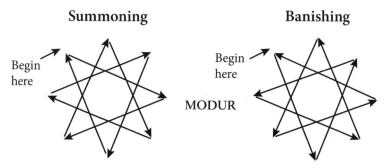

Figure 5–6: Octagrams of Modur

Second, standing at the west of the altar facing east, trace the summoning Octagram of Modur, as shown in figure 5–6, in the air above the altar using the first two fingers of your right hand. Imagine your fingers drawing the octagram in a line of brilliant red light. Then point to the center of the octagram and say the following, vibrating the name written in capital letters:

In the sacred name TARANIS and by the holy ash, I call upon the powers of Modur the Mover, the Fifth Sphere of the Tree of Life, to hallow and bless this ritual of Calan Gwyngalaf, and awaken for me the sixth station of Merlin's Wheel. Taranis of the thunders, mighty god of the Fifth Sphere, I pray that you will bless and guide me in this work of self-initiation.

Third, bow or curtsy to the divine presence you have invoked, and take your seat in the west. Read aloud the narrative of the season in a clear, slow voice:

Then Merlin said, "Dearer to me than the haunts of humankind is the wood, and there will I go and dwell." And he left the court of Arthur, and no one saw the manner of his leaving; and he journeyed to the forest of Caledon and to the place where the well of Galabes springs forth within a grove of great trees, and there he made his dwelling. All the wild things of that country knew him and feared him not; the deer gathered to his call, the wild boars watched their piglets play at his feet, and a wolf came from the northern moors to sit beside him and be his companion in the forest.

To him came messengers from the court of Arthur, and lastly his sister Ganieda, asking him to return, but he would not leave the wood, even as summer turned to winter. Finally there came to him Taliesin, the wisest of all the bards of Britain, who did not ask him to return, but conversed with him concerning the secrets of nature.

Fourth, meditate for a time on the narrative. Five or ten minutes of meditation should be a workable minimum at the Ovate stage of the work.

Fifth, rise from the chair and go to the west of the altar facing east. Standing there, trace the banishing Octagram of Modur, as shown in figure 5–6, in the air above the altar using the first two fingers of your right hand. Imagine your fingers drawing the octagram in a line of brilliant red light. Then point to the center of the octagram and say the following, vibrating the name written in capital letters:

In the sacred name TARANIS and by the holy ash tree, I thank the powers of Modur the Mover, the Fifth Sphere of the Tree of Life, for hallowing and blessing this ritual of Calan Gwyngalaf, and awakening for me the sixth station of Merlin's Wheel. Taranis of the thunders, mighty god of the Tenth Sphere, I thank you for your help in this work of self-initiation.

Sixth, bow or curtsy to the divine presence and then perform the complete closing ritual as given in chapter 4.

ALBAN ELFED, SEPTEMBER 22

Before starting, set up your working space as a temple. The altar is at the center with a blue altar cloth. On it are three white candles in candlesticks, a bowl or cauldron of water, and a bowl or cauldron of sand on which to burn incense; you may also, if you wish, put on the altar any seasonal decorations suitable to the place where you live. Place a chair in the west facing the altar. Sit there for a few moments of silence to calm your mind and focus on the ritual work you are about to do, then stand up, go to the altar, and begin.

First, perform the complete opening ritual as given in chapter 4.

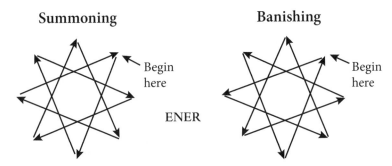

Figure 5–7: Octagrams of Ener

Second, standing at the west of the altar facing east, trace the summoning Octagram of Ener, as shown in figure 5–7, in the air above the altar using the first two fingers of your right hand. Imagine your fingers drawing the octagram in a line of sky-blue light. Then point to the center of the octagram and say the following, vibrating the name written in capital letters:

In the sacred name BELINUS and by the holy birch, I call upon the powers of Ener the Namer, the Fourth Sphere of the Tree of Life, to hallow and bless this ritual of Alban Elfed, and awaken for me the seventh station of Merlin's Wheel. Belinus, the Lord of the Year, god of the Fourth Sphere, I pray that you will bless and guide me in this work of self-initiation.

Third, bow or curtsy to the divine presence you have invoked, and take your seat in the west. Read aloud the narrative of the season in a clear, slow voice:

> Then Taliesin and Merlin went down among the fallen, and there found Arthur lying upon the grass, red with many wounds, and Bedwyr, the last of his warriors, kneeling beside him, all alone save Arthur and the dead. And Taliesin asked, "Does the king still live?" And Bedwyr answered, "He does, and when he goes to his grave so shall I."
>
> Then Merlin laughed and said, "Not wise the thought, a grave for Arthur! Be of good cheer and lift up your head, and you will behold a wonder." And Bedwyr looked, and a ship was coming toward the shore beside the field of battle. "That is the ship of Barinthus," said Merlin then, "who knows well the waters and the stars of heaven, and he shall bear Arthur to the Isle of Avalon, where Morgen the queen of that isle will heal him of his wounds. There shall he abide, king once and king to be, until he comes again."

Fourth, meditate for a time on the narrative. Five or ten minutes of meditation should be a workable minimum at the Ovate stage of the work.

Fifth, rise from the chair and go to the west of the altar facing east. Standing there, trace the banishing Octagram of Ener, as shown in figure 5–7, in the air above the altar using the first two fingers of your right hand. Imagine your fingers drawing the octagram in a line of sky-blue light. Then point to the center of the octagram and say the following, vibrating the name written in capital letters:

> In the sacred name BELINUS and by the holy birch, I thank the powers of Ener the Namer, the Fourth Sphere of the Tree of Life, for hallowing and blessing this ritual of Alban Elfed, and awakening for me the seventh station of Merlin's Wheel. Belinus, the Lord of the Year, great god of the Fourth Sphere, I thank you for your help in this work of self-initiation.

Sixth, bow or curtsy to the divine presence and then perform the complete closing ritual as given in chapter 4.

——— CALAN TACHWEDD, NOVEMBER 1 ———

Before starting, set up your working space as a temple. The altar is at the center with a black altar cloth. On it are three white candles in candlesticks, a bowl or cauldron of water, and a bowl or cauldron of sand on which to burn incense; you may also, if you wish, put on the altar any seasonal decorations suitable to the place where you live. Place a chair in the west facing the altar. Sit there for a few moments of silence to calm your mind and focus on the ritual work you are about to do, then stand up, go to the altar, and begin.

First, perform the complete opening ritual as given in chapter 4.

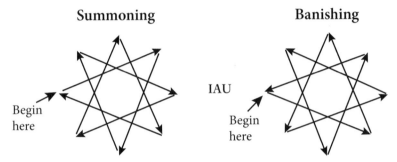

Figure 5–8: Octagrams of Iau

Second, standing at the west of the altar facing east, trace the summoning Octagram of Iau, as shown in figure 5–8, in the air above the altar using the first two fingers of your right hand. Imagine your fingers drawing the octagram in a line of pure white light. Then point to the center of the octagram and say the following, vibrating the name written in capital letters:

In the sacred name CERIDWEN and by the holy yew, I call upon the powers of Iau the Yoke, which reflects the three highest Spheres of the Tree of Life, to hallow and bless this ritual of Calan Tachwedd, and awaken for me the last station of Merlin's Wheel. Ceridwen the Wise, goddess of Iau, I pray that you will bless and guide me in this work of self-initiation.

Third, bow or curtsy to the divine presence you have invoked, and take your seat in the west. Read aloud the narrative of the season in a clear, slow voice:

And when Arthur was gone Merlin returned again to the forest of Caledon and to the well of Galabes, and dwelt there for many long years. To him came his sister Ganieda, who had been wed to one of the kings of that land and was now widowed, and she dwelt with him in the forest.

And Ganieda built for him beside the well of Galabes a chamber in which were seventy windows, so that through them he could see all the stars of heaven. And when it was done Merlin said to her and to Taliesin, "I shall now depart from among you and from all mortal beings, for it is my fate to go alive into the earth, and there remain." And he bid them farewell and went into the chamber that was prepared for him, and from there passed into the earth, nor has any mortal being seen him since that day.

Fourth, meditate for a time on the narrative. Five or ten minutes of meditation should be a workable minimum at the Ovate stage of the work.

Fifth, rise from the chair and go to the west of the altar facing east. Standing there, trace the banishing Octagram of Iau, as shown in figure 5–8, in the air above the altar using the first two fingers of your right hand. Imagine your fingers drawing the octagram in a line of pure white light. Then point to the center of the octagram and say the following, vibrating the name written in capital letters:

In the sacred name CERIDWEN and by the holy yew, I thank the powers of Iau the Yoke, which reflects the three highest Spheres of the Tree of Life, for hallowing and blessing this ritual of Calan Tachwedd, and awakening for me the last station of Merlin's Wheel. Ceridwen the Wise, goddess of the cauldron of Iau, I thank you for your help in this work of self-initiation.

Sixth, bow or curtsy to the divine presence and then perform the complete closing ritual as given in chapter 4.

CHAPTER SIX
THE BARDIC CIRCLE

With the rituals of the Bardic Circle, the mysteries of Merlin take on a greater degree of magical intensity. The pentagram rituals and the practice of Composition of Place make it possible for you to establish a stronger link to the inner energies that move through the Merlin legend, and the effects on your consciousness and your daily life will be correspondingly more potent. Even so, those effects will be measured precisely by the effort you put into the work before you and the work you have already done in the Ovate Circle.

Plan on spending a full year on the rituals of this level, building on the foundations you set in place during the work of the Ovate Circle and preparing yourself for the still more intensive rituals of the Druid Circle. The temptation to jump ahead is understandable, but it's also counterproductive. It's a waste of time trying to put the battlements on your magical tower until you've finished building the walls, just as it's a waste of effort to start building the walls until the foundation is in place. Take the process of self-initiation a step at a time and the results will be enduring.

—— ALBAN ARTHAN, DECEMBER 21 ——

Before starting, set up your working space as a temple. The altar is at the center with a brown altar cloth. On it are three white candles in candlesticks, a bowl or cauldron of water, and a bowl or cauldron of sand on which to burn incense; you may also, if you wish, put on the altar any seasonal decorations suitable to the place where you live. Place a chair in the west facing the altar. Sit there for a few moments of silence to calm your mind and focus on the ritual work you are about to do, then stand up, go to the altar, and begin.

First, perform the complete opening ritual.

Second, starting at the west of the altar facing east, perform the summoning pentagram ritual of earth. Return to the altar.

Third, standing at the west of the altar facing east, trace the summoning Octagram of Naf in the air above the altar using the first two fingers of your right hand. Imagine your fingers drawing the octagram in a line of indigo light. Then point to the center of the octagram and say the following, vibrating the name written in capital letters:

In the sacred name OLWEN and by the holy hawthorn, I call upon the powers of Naf the Shaper, the Tenth Sphere of the Tree of Life, to hallow and bless this ritual of Alban Arthan, and awaken for me the first station of Merlin's Wheel. Olwen of the White Track, maiden goddess of the Tenth Sphere, I pray that you will bless and guide me in this work of self-initiation.

Fourth, bow or curtsy to the divine presence you have invoked, and take your seat in the west. Then perform the Composition of Place, imagining as clearly as possible the following image as though it was physically present on the other side of the altar.

Beneath the branches of a leafless hawthorn tree sits a young woman dressed in a plain dress of rough brown cloth, tied at the waist with a rope belt. Her legs are folded beneath her, her feet are bare, and her hair is long and brown. She wears no ornaments. In her arms is a baby boy, Merlin the infant, wrapped in a coarse, brown woolen blanket. She looks down lovingly at the child's face, but the child looks out at you and his bright eyes sparkle with intelligence. In the background, the door of a hermitage opens into the side of a hill. Forest trees surround the scene and a cold wind keens in their bare branches.

Fifth, read aloud the narrative of the season in a clear, slow voice:

The king asked her, "Who is the father of your child?" And the princess answered, "I know not. All I know is that when I dwelt in my father's house with my maidens, one night while I slept, there appeared to me one in the form of a handsome young man who spoke to me and kissed me, then vanished so that I could no longer see him. Often thereafter he came to me, sometimes visibly and sometimes not, and at length he lay beside me and made love to me as a man would, and after that I found that I was with child. Now you must decide what this child's father was, for apart from that, I have never been with a man."

And the king sent for Magan the wise, his counselor, and when Magan had heard the whole story he said, "In the books of the sages it is written that many a child has been born in this way. For there are a race of spirits who dwell between the earth and the moon who are partly of the nature of men and partly of the nature of angels, and when they wish they can assume mortal form and cohabit with human beings. It is possible that one of these appeared to this woman and begot the child upon her."

Sixth, meditate for a time on the energies of the season. Ten to fifteen minutes of meditation is a workable minimum for the Bardic stage of the work.

Seventh, dissolve the Composition of Place.

Eighth, rise from the chair and go to the west of the altar facing east. Standing there, trace the banishing Octagram of Naf in the air above the altar using the first two fingers of your right hand. Imagine your fingers drawing the octagram in a line of indigo light. Then point to the center of the octagram and say the following, vibrating the name written in capital letters:

In the sacred name OLWEN and by the holy hawthorn, I thank the powers of Naf the Shaper, the Tenth Sphere of the Tree of Life, for hallowing and blessing this ritual of Alban Arthan, and awakening for me the first station of Merlin's Wheel. Olwen of the White Track, maiden goddess of the Tenth Sphere, I thank you for your help in this work of self-initiation.

Ninth, perform the banishing pentagram ritual of earth.
Tenth, perform the complete closing ritual.

──── CALAN MYRI, FEBRUARY 2 ────

Before starting, set up your working space as a temple. The altar is at the center with a violet altar cloth. On it are three white candles in candlesticks, a bowl or cauldron of water, and a bowl or cauldron of sand on which to burn incense; you may also, if you wish, put on the altar any seasonal decorations suitable to the place where you live. Place a chair in the west facing the altar. Sit there for a few moments of silence to calm your mind and focus on the ritual work you are about to do, then stand up, go to the altar, and begin.

First, perform the complete opening ritual.

Second, starting at the west of the altar facing east, perform the summoning pentagram ritual of earth. Return to the altar.

Third, standing at the west of the altar facing east, trace the summoning Octagram of Ner in the air above the altar using the first two fingers of your right hand. Imagine your fingers drawing the octagram in a line of violet light. Then point to the center of the octagram and say the invocation below. As noted already, the name that you vibrate should be the one of the opposite gender to that of your physical body to establish a polarity between you and the deity—thus men should vibrate the name Sul (pronounced "SEEL"), while women vibrate the name Coel (pronounced "CO-ell").

In the sacred name (SUL or COEL) and by the holy willow, I call upon the powers of Ner the Mighty, the Ninth Sphere of the Tree of Life, to hallow and bless this ritual of Calan Myri, and awaken for me the second station of Merlin's Wheel. Sul of the healing Springs (or) Coel the master of the wild places, goddess (or) god of the Ninth Sphere, I pray that you will bless and guide me in this work of self-initiation.

Fourth, bow or curtsy to the divine presence you have invoked, and take your seat in the west. Then perform the Composition of Place, imagining as clearly as possible the following image as though it was physically present on the other side of the altar.

A king dressed in purple robes and wearing a golden crown sits on the edge of an empty pool in a cavern. He has black hair and a short, neatly trimmed black beard. Beside him stands a young brown-haired boy,

Merlin the child, barefoot and bareheaded, dressed in a simple sleeveless tunic of unbleached linen. The child is pointing with one hand at the air before them where two mighty dragons, one red and the other white, coil around each other in a double helix, clawing each other as they rise up into the air together. The ground shakes beneath the king and the child, and the roar of flames as the dragons spit fire at each other fills the air.

Fifth, read aloud the narrative of the season in a clear, slow voice:

Then the boy spoke to King Vortigern, saying, "Your wise men have lied to you, for they do not know what lies beneath this hill. Command your servants to dig and they will find a pool hidden beneath the ground. Let them dig channels and drain away the water and then a marvel will be seen. For beneath the water lie two hollow stones, and under the stones lie two great dragons, and it is they who will not permit your tower to stand."

So the king commanded his servants to dig, and soon they discovered the pool and marveled at the boy's wisdom. They dug channels and drained away the water and found the two hollow stones. Then the king sat beside the empty pool and watched, and the two dragons came forth from the hollow stones. One of them was white and the other red, and they leapt upon each other, biting and clawing and breathing fire, so that no struggle so fierce had ever been seen in that land. Then the king turned to the boy and asked him what the combat between the dragons meant. At once Merlin burst into tears and began to prophesy.

Sixth, meditate for a time on the energies of the season. Ten to fifteen minutes of meditation is a workable minimum for the Bardic stage of the work.

Seventh, dissolve the Composition of Place.

Eighth, rise from the chair and go to the west of the altar facing east. Standing there, trace the banishing Octagram of Ner in the air above the altar using the first two fingers of your right hand. Imagine your fingers drawing the octagram in a line of indigo light. Then point to the center of the octagram and say the following, vibrating the name written in capital letters:

In the sacred name (SUL or COEL) and by the holy willow, I thank the powers of Ner the Mighty, the Ninth Sphere of the Tree of Life, for hallowing and blessing this ritual of Calan Myri, and awakening for me the second station of Merlin's Wheel. Sul of the healing springs (or) Coel the master of the wild places, goddess (or) god of the Ninth Sphere, I thank you for your help in this work of self-initiation.

Ninth, perform the banishing pentagram ritual of earth.
Tenth, perform the complete closing ritual.

——— ALBAN EILIR, MARCH 21 ———

Before starting, set up your working space as a temple. The altar is at the center with an orange altar cloth. On it are three white candles in candlesticks, a bowl or cauldron of water, and a bowl or cauldron of sand on which to burn incense; you may also, if you wish, put on the altar any seasonal decorations suitable to the place where you live. Place a chair in the west facing the altar. Sit there for a few moments of silence to calm your mind and focus on the ritual work you are about to do, then stand up, go to the altar, and begin.

First, perform the complete opening ritual.

Second, starting at the west of the altar facing east, perform the summoning pentagram ritual of air. Return to the altar.

Third, standing at the west of the altar facing east, trace the summoning Octagram of Byth in the air above the altar using the first two fingers of your right hand. Imagine your fingers drawing the octagram in a line of orange light. Then point to the center of the octagram and say the following, vibrating the name written in capital letters:

In the sacred name MABON and by the holy hazel, I call upon the powers of Byth the Eternal, the Eighth Sphere of the Tree of Life, to hallow and bless this ritual of Alban Eilir, and awaken for me the third station of Merlin's Wheel. Mabon, son of Modron, ever-young god of the Eighth Sphere, I pray that you will bless and guide me in this work of self-initiation.

Fourth, bow or curtsy to the divine presence you have invoked, and take your seat in the west. Then perform the Composition of Place, imagining as clearly as possible the following image as though it was physically present on the other side of the altar.

A circle of standing stones, blue-gray in color, rises from a wide plain beneath a blue sky dotted with clouds. In the center of the circle stands a brown-haired lad, Merlin the boy, who wears a cloak and trousers the same color as the stones, a tunic of unbleached linen, and leather shoes. His head is bare, and his eyes are blue and piercing. All around, just

outside the circle of stones, stands a great concourse of people, the men
in tunics, cloaks, and trousers, the women in cloaks and long dresses,
watching him and murmuring in amazement.

Fifth, read aloud the narrative of the season in a clear, slow voice:

And Merlin said to Aurelius, "If you wish a fitting monument, let the stones of the Giants' Dance in the uttermost west be brought here and set in a ring. For those stones were brought from distant places and hallowed by secret rites in the most ancient times, and each one has healing powers." This counsel seemed good to Aurelius, and he sent his brother Uther and a great host of men and Merlin to bring back the stones of the Giants' Dance.

And when they had driven off the guardians of the stones, Uther and his men tried to draw the stones from the earth to bear them back to Britain, but they could not make a single stone yield to all their efforts. Then Merlin laughed, set out such gear as he needed, and easily drew up the stones and conveyed them to the ships, and they brought the stones back to the plain of Salisbury with great rejoicing. There, by Merlin's art, the great stones were set up in a mighty ring, and there the people of Britain made festival, and there Aurelius was crowned King of the Britons.

Sixth, meditate for a time on the energies of the season. Ten to fifteen minutes of meditation is a workable minimum for the Bardic stage of the work.

Seventh, dissolve the Composition of Place.

Eighth, rise from the chair and go to the west of the altar facing east. Standing there, trace the banishing Octagram of Byth in the air above the altar using the first two fingers of your right hand. Imagine your fingers drawing the octagram in a line of orange light. Then point to the center of the octagram and say the following, vibrating the name written in capital letters:

In the sacred name MABON and by the holy hazel, I thank the powers of Byth the Eternal, the Eighth Sphere of the Tree of Life, for hallowing and blessing this ritual of Alban Eilir, and awakening for me the third station of Merlin's Wheel. Mabon, son of Modron, ever-young god of the Eighth Sphere, I thank you for your help in this work of self-initiation.

Ninth, perform the banishing pentagram ritual of air.
Tenth, perform the complete closing ritual.

—— CALAN MAI, MAY 1 ——

Before starting, set up your working space as a temple. The altar is at the center with a green altar cloth. On it are three white candles in candlesticks, a bowl or cauldron of water, and a bowl or cauldron of sand on which to burn incense; you may also, if you wish, put on the altar any seasonal decorations suitable to the place where you live. Place a chair in the west facing the altar. Sit there for a few moments of silence to calm your mind and focus on the ritual work you are about to do, then stand up, go to the altar, and begin.

First, perform the complete opening ritual.

Second, starting at the west of the altar facing east, perform the summoning pentagram ritual of air. Return to the altar.

Third, standing at the west of the altar facing east, trace the summoning Octagram of Byw in the air above the altar using the first two fingers of your right hand. Imagine your fingers drawing the octagram in a line of emerald-green light. Then point to the center of the octagram and say the following, vibrating the name written in capital letters:

In the sacred name ELEN and by the holy apple tree, I call upon the powers of Byw the Living, the Seventh Sphere of the Tree of Life, to hallow and bless this ritual of Calan Mai, and awaken for me the fourth station of Merlin's Wheel. Elen of the roads and the twilight, goddess of the Seventh Sphere, I pray that you will bless and guide me in this work of self-initiation.

Fourth, bow or curtsy to the divine presence you have invoked, and take your seat in the west. Then perform the Composition of Place, imagining as clearly as possible the following image as though it was physically present on the other side of the altar.

A narrow beach of sand stretches between a rocky shore and the rolling waves of the gray sea; the rhythmic rushing of the waves on the beach is heard, and the air is tinged with salt spray. On the shore stands a young man, Merlin the youth, wearing a tunic of unbleached linen, trousers of brown cloth, and a green cloak. His hair is brown and long, and blows in the wind. Before him stands an old woman dressed in the greens and browns and grays of earth who holds a newborn child wrapped in a crimson cloak. The woman is giving the child to Merlin. Above the shore, a castle raises its battlements against a sky at sunrise.

Fifth, read aloud the narrative of the season in a clear, slow voice:

And King Uther said to Merlin, "Give me one night of love with the lady Ygerna, and in return I will give you whatever you will ask." And Merlin replied to him, "So be it." And he changed Uther's appearance to that of Ygerna's husband the Duke of Cornwall. That night Uther rode to the castle of Tintagel and Ygerna received him lovingly, thinking he was her husband. That night was Arthur the Pendragon conceived, and that same night the Duke of Cornwall died.

When nine months had passed and Ygerna gave birth to an infant boy, Merlin went to Uther and said, "When I brought you to Ygerna you promised me whatever I would ask. I ask now for the child you begot upon her." And the king commanded the nursemaid to take the infant to Merlin, who waited beside the sea. And he took Arthur to a hidden place where he was fostered with a worthy family and did not know his birth or his heritage.

Sixth, meditate for a time on the energies of the season. Ten to fifteen minutes of meditation is a workable minimum for the Bardic stage of the work.

Seventh, dissolve the Composition of Place.

Eighth, rise from the chair and go to the west of the altar facing east. Standing there, trace the banishing Octagram of Byw in the air above the altar using the first two fingers of your right hand. Imagine your fingers drawing the octagram in a line of emerald-green light. Then point to the center of the octagram and say the following, vibrating the name written in capital letters:

In the sacred name ELEN and by the holy apple tree, I thank the powers of Byw the Living, the Seventh Sphere of the Tree of Life, for hallowing and blessing this ritual of Calan Mai, and awakening for me the fourth station of Merlin's Wheel. Elen of the roads and the twilight, maiden goddess of the Tenth Sphere, I thank you for your help in this work of self-initiation.

Ninth, perform the banishing pentagram ritual of air.
Tenth, perform the complete closing ritual.

───── ALBAN HEFIN, JUNE 21 ─────

Before starting, set up your working space as a temple. The altar is at the center with a gold altar cloth. On it are three white candles in candlesticks, a bowl or cauldron of water, and a bowl or cauldron of sand on which to burn incense; you may also, if you wish, put on the altar any seasonal decorations suitable to the place where you live. Place a chair in the west facing the altar. Sit there for a few moments of silence to calm your mind and focus on the ritual work you are about to do, then stand up, go to the altar, and begin.

First, perform the complete opening ritual.

Second, starting at the west of the altar facing east, perform the summoning pentagram ritual of fire. Return to the altar.

Third, standing at the west of the altar facing east, trace the summoning Octagram of Muner in the air above the altar using the first two fingers of your right hand. Imagine your fingers drawing the octagram in a line of golden light. Then point to the center of the octagram and say the following, vibrating the name written in capital letters:

> In the sacred name ESUS and by the holy oak, I call upon the powers of Muner the Lord, the Sixth Sphere of the Tree of Life, to hallow and bless this ritual of Alban Hefin, and awaken for me the fifth station of Merlin's Wheel. Esus, chief of tree-spirits, god of the Sixth Sphere, I pray that you will bless and guide me in this work of self-initiation.

Fourth, bow or curtsy to the divine presence you have invoked, and take your seat in the west. Then perform the Composition of Place, imagining as clearly as possible the following image as though it was physically present on the other side of the altar.

The same circle of standing stones, blue-gray in color, stands on the plain, but now the plain is covered with flowers and the midsummer sun stands high in the heavens. In the center of the circle stands a tall figure, Merlin the young man, clad in robes of gold. His hair is brown, bound by a golden circlet, and he wears a short, brown beard. In both his hands he holds a golden crown upraised. Before him kneels a golden-haired youth in a coat of chain mail with a sword belted about his waist. The youth's head is bare. All around the circle gathers a great crowd of people of every station: great lords and ladies in robes and mantles trimmed with fur, warriors in coats of chain mail, and the common folk of the land in their brightly colored best clothing, all raising a shout of acclamation as Merlin places the crown on Arthur's head.

Fifth, read aloud the narrative of the season in a clear, slow voice:

Then Arthur once more lightly drew the sword out of the stone. But the barons said, "Who is this youth that he should reign over us?" And Merlin answered them, "This is Arthur, who is the son of Uther Pendragon. By right of blood, as also by right of drawing the sword from the stone as you have seen this day, he is to be King of the Britons." This the barons would not allow. But when word went forth that the barons still refused their homage to Arthur, the common people of the country rose up as one and said, "We will have Arthur as our king, and he who would deny him the crown, him we will slay."

So the barons knelt before Arthur and did him homage, and Merlin anointed him and placed the crown that had been his father's upon his head. And so did Arthur become King of the Britons, and long held the realm of Logres in peace.

Sixth, meditate for a time on the energies of the season. Ten to fifteen minutes of meditation is a workable minimum for the Bardic stage of the work.

Seventh, dissolve the Composition of Place.

Eighth, rise from the chair and go to the west of the altar facing east. Standing there, trace the banishing Octagram of Muner in the air above the altar using the first two fingers of your right hand. Imagine your fingers drawing the octagram in a line of golden light. Then point to the center of the octagram and say the following, vibrating the name written in capital letters:

In the sacred name ESUS and by the holy oak, I thank the powers of Muner the Lord, the Sixth Sphere of the Tree of Life, for hallowing and blessing this ritual of Alban Hefin, and awakening for me the fifth station of Merlin's Wheel. Esus, chief of tree-spirits, god of the Sixth Sphere, I thank you for your help in this work of self-initiation.

Ninth, perform the banishing pentagram ritual of fire.
Tenth, perform the complete closing ritual.

———— CALAN GWYNGALAF, AUGUST I ————

Before starting, set up your working space as a temple. The altar is at the center with a red altar cloth. On it are three white candles in candlesticks, a bowl or cauldron of water, and a bowl or cauldron of sand on which to burn incense; you may also, if you wish, put on the altar any seasonal decorations suitable to the place where you live. Place a chair in the west facing the altar. Sit there for a few moments of silence to calm your mind and focus on the ritual work you are about to do, then stand up, go to the altar, and begin.

First, perform the complete opening ritual.

Second, starting at the west of the altar facing east, perform the summoning pentagram ritual of fire. Return to the altar.

Third, standing at the west of the altar facing east, trace the summoning Octagram of Modur in the air above the altar using the first two fingers of your right hand. Imagine your fingers drawing the octagram in a line of brilliant red light. Then point to the center of the octagram and say the following, vibrating the name written in capital letters:

In the sacred name TARANIS and by the holy ash tree, I call upon the powers of Modur the Mover, the Fifth Sphere of the Tree of Life, to hallow and bless this ritual of Calan Gwyngalaf, and awaken for me the sixth station of Merlin's Wheel. Taranis of the thunders, mighty god of the Fifth Sphere, I pray that you will bless and guide me in this work of self-initiation.

Fourth, bow or curtsy to the divine presence you have invoked, and take your seat in the west. Then perform the Composition of Place, imagining as clearly as possible the following image as though it was physically present on the other side of the altar.

A great oak rises in the midst of dense forest. At the foot of the oak is an outcropping of gray stone, and from a cleft in the stone a spring bubbles up, giving birth to a narrow stream that flows away. Other trees press close all around and sunlight filtered through their leaves dapples the ground; the song of birds is everywhere, and deer, boars, and other wild things move through the forest. Beside the spring, sitting with his back to the oak, is Merlin, the man of middle years, his beard long and his brown hair unkempt. He is wrapped in a cloak the orange color of autumn leaves, and he gazes down into the waters of the spring as though he sees something there that other eyes do not see. Beside him sits a gray wolf, its tongue lolling; Merlin's hand rests on the wolf's back.

Fifth, read aloud the narrative of the season in a clear, slow voice:

Then Merlin said, "Dearer to me than the haunts of humankind is the wood, and there will I go and dwell." And he left the court of Arthur, and no one saw the manner of his leaving; and he journeyed to the forest of Caledon and to the place where the well of Galabes springs forth within a grove of great trees, and there he made his dwelling. All the wild things of that country knew him and feared him not; the deer gathered to his call, the wild boars watched their piglets play at his feet, and a wolf came from the northern moors to sit beside him and be his companion in the forest.

To him came messengers from the court of Arthur, and lastly his sister Ganieda, asking him to return, but he would not leave the wood, even as summer turned to winter. Finally there came to him Taliesin, the wisest of all the bards of Britain, who did not ask him to return, but conversed with him concerning the secrets of nature.

Sixth, meditate for a time on the energies of the season. Ten to fifteen minutes of meditation is a workable minimum for the Bardic stage of the work.

Seventh, dissolve the Composition of Place.

Eighth, rise from the chair and go to the west of the altar facing east. Standing there, trace the banishing Octagram of Modur in the air above the altar using the first two fingers of your right hand. Imagine your fingers drawing the octagram in a line of brilliant red light. Then point to the center of the octagram and say the following, vibrating the name written in capital letters:

In the sacred name TARANIS and by the holy ash tree, I thank the powers of Modur the Mover, the Fifth Sphere of the Tree of Life, for hallowing and blessing this ritual of Calan Gwyngalaf, and awakening for me the sixth station of Merlin's Wheel. Taranis of the thunders, mighty god of the Fifth Sphere, I thank you for your help in this work of self-initiation.

Ninth, perform the banishing pentagram ritual of air.
Tenth, perform the complete closing ritual.

——— ALBAN ELFED, SEPTEMBER 22 ———

Before starting, set up your working space as a temple. The altar is at the center with a blue altar cloth. On it are three white candles in candlesticks, a bowl or cauldron of water, and a bowl or cauldron of sand on which to burn incense; you may also, if you wish, put on the altar any seasonal decorations suitable to the place where you live. Place a chair in the west facing the altar. Sit there for a few moments of silence to calm your mind and focus on the ritual work you are about to do, then stand up, go to the altar, and begin.

First, perform the complete opening ritual.

Second, starting at the west of the altar facing east, perform the summoning pentagram ritual of water. Return to the altar.

Third, standing at the west of the altar facing east, trace the summoning Octagram of Ener in the air above the altar using the first two fingers of your right hand. Imagine your fingers drawing the octagram in a line of sky-blue light. Then point to the center of the octagram and say the following, vibrating the name written in capital letters:

In the sacred name BELINUS and by the holy birch, I call upon the powers of Ener the Namer, the Fourth Sphere of the Tree of Life, to hallow and bless this ritual of Alban Elfed, and awaken for me the seventh station of Merlin's Wheel. Belinus, the Lord of the Year, god of the Fourth Sphere, I pray that you will bless and guide me in this work of self-initiation.

Fourth, bow or curtsy to the divine presence you have invoked, and take your seat in the west. Then perform the Composition of Place, imagining as clearly as possible the following image as though it was physically present on the other side of the altar.

A grassy shore slopes down to the sea. On the shore stand three men, and beside them a fourth lies on the grass. To the left is Taliesin, a youthful man with black hair, dressed in robes of blue, green, and white; he has a harp cradled in one arm. To the right is Bedwyr, a middle-aged man with blond hair going to gray, wearing a battered coat of chain mail, an iron helmet that does not cover his face, and leather hose; he has a sword hanging from a belt around his waist. To one side lies Arthur, wearing armor like Bedwyr's; his face is pale, his hair and beard golden, and his coat of mail is hacked and stained with blood. In the center is Merlin the old man. He wears a great cloak of crimson red and a long white robe; his arms are upraised; his hair and beard, both long, are gray. In the distance, beneath a blue autumn sky scattered with clouds, a ship with a single square sail draws near.

Fifth, read aloud the narrative of the season in a clear, slow voice:

Then Taliesin and Merlin went down among the fallen, and there found Arthur lying upon the grass, red with many wounds, and Bedwyr, the last of his warriors, kneeling beside him, all alone save Arthur and the dead. And Taliesin asked, "Does the king still live?" And Bedwyr answered, "He does, and when he goes to his grave so shall I."

Then Merlin laughed and said, "Not wise the thought, a grave for Arthur! Be of good cheer and lift up your head, and you will behold a wonder." And Bedwyr looked, and a ship was coming toward the shore beside the field of battle. "That is the ship of Barinthus," said Merlin then, "who knows well the waters and the stars of heaven, and he shall bear Arthur to the Isle of Avalon, where Morgen the queen of that isle will heal him of his wounds. There shall he abide, king once and king to be, until he comes again."

Sixth, meditate for a time on the energies of the season. Ten to fifteen minutes of meditation is a workable minimum for the Bardic stage of the work.

Seventh, dissolve the Composition of Place.

Eighth, rise from the chair and go to the west of the altar facing east. Standing there, trace the banishing Octagram of Ener in the air above the altar using the first two fingers of your right hand. Imagine your fingers drawing the octagram in a line of sky-blue light. Then point to the center of the octagram and say the following, vibrating the name written in capital letters:

In the sacred name BELINUS and by the holy birch, I thank the powers of Ener the Namer, the Fourth Sphere of the Tree of Life, for hallowing and blessing this ritual of Alban Elfed, and awakening for me the seventh station of Merlin's Wheel. Belinus, the Lord of the Year, great god of the Fourth Sphere, I thank you for your help in this work of self-initiation.

Ninth, perform the banishing pentagram ritual of water.
Tenth, perform the complete closing ritual.

───── CALAN TACHWEDD, NOVEMBER 1 ─────

Before starting, set up your working space as a temple. The altar is at the center with a black altar cloth. On it are three white candles in candlesticks, a bowl or cauldron of water, and a bowl or cauldron of sand on which to burn incense; you may also, if you wish, put on the altar any seasonal decorations suitable to the place where you live. Place a chair in the west facing the altar. Sit there for a few moments of silence to calm your mind and focus on the ritual work you are about to do, then stand up, go to the altar, and begin.

First, perform the complete opening ritual.

Second, starting at the west of the altar facing east, perform the summoning pentagram ritual of water. Return to the altar.

Third, standing at the west of the altar facing east, trace the summoning Octagram of Iau in the air above the altar using the first two fingers of your right hand. Imagine your fingers drawing the octagram in a line of pure white light. Then point to the center of the octagram and say the following, vibrating the name written in capital letters:

In the sacred name CERIDWEN and by the holy yew, I call upon the powers of Iau the Yoke, which reflects the three highest Spheres of the Tree of Life, to hallow and bless this ritual of Calan Tachwedd, and awaken for me the last station of Merlin's Wheel. Ceridwen the Wise, goddess of Iau, I pray that you will bless and guide me in this work of self-initiation.

Fourth, bow or curtsy to the divine presence you have invoked, and take your seat in the west. Then perform the Composition of Place, imagining as clearly as possible the following image as though it was physically present on the other side of the altar.

In a forest grove in autumn, tall oaks rise high above a forest floor covered with brown fallen leaves, and a few leaves still cling to the branches above. In the midst of the grove stands a newly made earthen mound with a low door that faces you, opening into utter darkness. Two tall stones flank the door, carved in spiral patterns. In front of the door stands Merlin the ancient, his hair and beard white, wearing a plain white robe. To his right stands an old woman dressed in black, her hair gray, her face resembling Merlin's. To his left stands Taliesin in his robes of green, blue, and white. Merlin extends one hand to each of them and they each hold his hand in both of theirs as they say their farewells.

Fifth, read aloud the narrative of the season in a clear, slow voice:

And when Arthur was gone Merlin returned again to the forest of Caledon and to the well of Galabes. To him came his sister Ganieda, who had been wed to one of the kings of that land and was now widowed, and she dwelt with him in the forest.

And Ganieda built for him beside the well of Galabes a chamber in which were seventy windows, so that through them he could see all the stars of heaven. And when it was done Merlin said to her and to Taliesin, "I shall now depart from among you and from all mortal beings, for it is my fate to go alive into the earth, and there remain." And he bid them farewell and went into the chamber that was prepared for him, and from there passed into the earth, nor has any mortal being seen him since that day.

Sixth, meditate for a time on the energies of the season. Ten to fifteen minutes of meditation is a workable minimum for the Bardic stage of the work.

Seventh, dissolve the Composition of Place.

Eighth, rise from the chair and go to the west of the altar facing east. Standing there, trace the banishing Octagram of Iau in the air above the altar using the first two fingers of your right hand. Imagine your fingers drawing the octagram in a line of pure white light. Then point to the center of the octagram and say the following, vibrating the name written in capital letters:

In the sacred name CERIDWEN and by the holy yew, I thank the powers of Iau the Yoke, which reflects the three highest Spheres of the Tree of Life, for hallowing and blessing this ritual of Calan Tachwedd, and awakening for me the last station of Merlin's Wheel. Ceridwen the Wise, goddess of the cauldron of Iau, I thank you for your help in this work of self-initiation.

Ninth, perform the banishing pentagram ritual of water.
Tenth, perform the complete closing ritual.

—— Chapter Seven ——
The Druid Circle

With the ceremonies of the Druid Circle, the preparations are finished and the mysteries of Merlin's Wheel can be practiced in their complete form. The octagram rituals summon and banish the energies of the spheres of the Tree of Life; the consecration of mead for offering and communion enable you to bring the energies of the working into your body in a more intensive form than the Ovate and Bardic Circle ceremonies permit. Combined with the rituals and practices you have learned in the two previous circles, these open the portals to self-initiation.

Plan on spending at least one year working the ceremonies of the Druid Circle. Once you have done so, an important choice awaits you. Up to this point you have been one of the *mystai* of the mysteries of Merlin; now you must decide whether to go on to become one of the *epoptai*, the initiates who continue to participate in the ceremonies after their initiation and gain the deeper dimensions of initiation that come from that experience. If you do, you will find—as the *epoptai* of the Eleusinian mysteries found in ancient times, and as members of other initiatory orders have found over and over again since that time—that repeated participation in a set of initiatory rites opens up portal after portal. Still, you and you alone can decide whether this choice is right for you.

──── ALBAN ARTHAN, DECEMBER 21 ────

Before starting, set up your working space as a temple. The altar is at the center with a brown altar cloth. On it are three white candles in candlesticks, a bowl or cauldron of water, a bowl or cauldron of sand on which to burn incense, and the cup or horn of mead; you may also, if you wish, put on the altar any seasonal decorations suitable to the place where you live. Place a chair in the west facing the altar. Sit there for a few moments of silence to calm your mind and focus on the ritual work you are about to do, then stand up, go to the altar, and begin.

First, perform the complete opening ritual.

Second, starting at the west of the altar facing east, perform the summoning octagram ritual of Naf, vibrating the name OLWEN in each quarter. Return to the altar.

Third, take your seat in the west. Then perform the Composition of Place, imagining as clearly as possible the following image as though it was physically present on the other side of the altar.

Beneath the leafless branches of a hawthorn tree sits a young woman dressed in a plain dress of rough brown cloth, tied at the waist with a rope belt. Her legs are folded beneath her, her feet are bare, and her hair is long and brown. She wears no ornaments. In her arms is a baby boy, Merlin the infant, wrapped in a coarse, brown woolen blanket. She looks down lovingly at the child's face, but the child looks out at you and his bright eyes sparkle with intelligence. In the background, the door of a hermitage opens into the side of a hill. Forest trees surround the scene and a cold wind keens in their bare branches.

Fourth, read aloud the narrative of the season in a clear, slow voice:

The king asked her, "Who is the father of your child?" And the princess answered, "I know not. All I know is that when I dwelt in my father's house with my maidens, one night while I slept, there appeared to me one in the form of a handsome young man who spoke to me and kissed me, then vanished so that I could no longer see him. Often thereafter he came to me, sometimes visibly and sometimes not, and at length he lay beside me and made love to me as a man would, and after that I found that I was with child. Now you must decide what this child's father was, for apart from that, I have never been with a man."

And the king sent for Magan the wise, his counselor, and when Magan had heard the whole story he said, "In the books of the sages it is written that many a child has been born in this way. For there are a race of spirits who dwell between the earth and the moon who are partly of the nature of men and partly of the nature of angels, and when they wish they can assume mortal form and cohabit with human beings. It is possible that one of these appeared to this woman and begot the child upon her."

Fifth, rise and go to the altar. Standing at the west of the altar facing east, trace the summoning Octagram of Naf in the air above the cup or horn of mead on the altar using the first two fingers of your right hand. Imagine your fingers drawing the octagram in a line of indigo light. Then point to the center of the octagram and say the following, vibrating the name written in capital letters:

In the sacred name OLWEN and by the holy hawthorn, I call upon the powers of Naf the Shaper, the Tenth Sphere of the Tree of Life, to hallow and bless this ritual of Alban Arthan, to awaken for me the first station of Merlin's Wheel, and to consecrate to this purpose this offering of mead. Olwen of the White Track, maiden goddess of the Tenth Sphere, aid me in calling down the light that was before the worlds in this season of Alban Arthan.

Now perform the OIW Analysis, reciting the words and making the gestures given in chapter 4. Call down light from infinite space above you into the cup or horn of mead, transforming the mead into pure light.

Then release the image and lift up the cup or horn of mead in both hands. Say: "Olwen, maiden goddess, receive this offering as I receive your blessing." Pour out some of the mead onto the ground or into the offering bowl. Then raise the cup or horn again and drink the remainder, letting it bring the energies of the season into you.

Sixth, sit in the west and meditate for a time on the energies of the season. Pursue the meditation for as long as you keep finding new insights. You may find it useful to take notes and meditate further on the ritual in the following days.

Seventh, dissolve the Composition of Place.

Eighth, rise from the chair and go to the west of the altar facing east. Standing there, trace the banishing Octagram of Naf in the air above the altar using the first two fingers of your right hand. Imagine your fingers drawing the octagram in a line of indigo light. Then point to the center of the octagram and say the following, vibrating the name written in capital letters:

In the sacred name OLWEN and by the holy hawthorn, I thank the powers of Naf the Shaper, the Tenth Sphere of the Tree of Life, for hallowing and blessing this ritual of Alban Arthan, and awakening for me the first station of Merlin's Wheel. Olwen of the White Track, maiden goddess of the Tenth Sphere, I thank you for your help in this work of self-initiation.

Ninth, perform the banishing octagram ritual of Naf.

Tenth, perform the complete closing ritual.

———— CALAN MYRI, FEBRUARY 2 ————

Before starting, set up your working space as a temple. The altar is at the center with a violet altar cloth. On it are three white candles in candlesticks, a bowl or cauldron of water, a bowl or cauldron of sand on which to burn incense, and the cup or horn of mead; you may also, if you wish, put on the altar any seasonal decorations suitable to the place where you live. Place a chair in the west facing the altar. Sit there for a few moments of silence to calm your mind and focus on the ritual work you are about to do, then stand up, go to the altar, and begin.

First, perform the complete opening ritual.

Second, starting at the west of the altar facing east, perform the summoning octagram ritual of Ner, vibrating the appropriate divine name in each quarter. As already discussed, the name that you vibrate should be the one of the opposite gender to that of your physical body to establish a polarity between you and the deity—thus men should vibrate the name Sul (pronounced "SEEL"), while women vibrate the name Coel (pronounced "CO-ell"). Return to the altar.

Third, take your seat in the west. Then perform the Composition of Place as follows, imagining as clearly as possible the following image as though it was physically present on the other side of the altar.

A king dressed in purple robes and wearing a golden crown sits on the edge of an empty pool in a cavern. He has black hair and a short, neatly trimmed black beard. Beside him stands a young brown-haired boy, Merlin the child, barefoot and bareheaded, dressed in a simple sleeveless tunic of unbleached linen. The child is pointing with one hand at the air before them where two mighty dragons, one red and the other white, coil around each other in a double helix, clawing each other as they rise up into the air together. The ground shakes beneath the king and the child, and the roar of flames as the dragons spit fire at each other fills the air.

Fourth, read aloud the narrative of the season in a clear, slow voice:

Then the boy spoke to King Vortigern, saying: "Your wise men have lied to you, for they do not know what lies beneath this hill. Command your servants to dig and they will find a pool hidden beneath the ground. Let them dig channels and drain away the water and then a marvel will be seen. For beneath the water lie two hollow stones, and under the stones lie two great dragons, and it is they who will not permit your tower to stand."

So the king commanded his servants to dig, and soon they discovered the pool and marveled at the boy's wisdom. They dug channels and drained away the water and found the two hollow stones. Then the king sat beside the empty pool and watched, and the two dragons came forth from the hollow stones. One of them was white and the other red, and they leapt upon each other, biting and clawing and breathing fire, so that no struggle so fierce had ever been seen in that land. Then the king turned to the boy and asked him what the combat between the dragons meant. At once Merlin burst into tears and began to prophesy.

Fifth, rise and go to the altar. Standing at the west of the altar facing east, trace the summoning Octagram of Ner in the air above the cup or horn of mead on the altar using the first two fingers of your right hand. Imagine your fingers drawing the octagram in a line of violet light. Then point to the center of the octagram and say the following:

In the sacred name (SUL or COEL) and by the holy willow, I call upon the powers of Ner the Mighty, the Ninth Sphere of the Tree of Life, to hallow and bless this ritual of Calan Myri, to awaken for me the second station of Merlin's Wheel, and to consecrate to this purpose this offering of mead. Sul of the healing Springs (or) Coel the master of the wild places, goddess (or) god of the Ninth Sphere, aid me in calling down the light that was before the worlds in this season of Calan Myri.

Now perform the OIW Analysis, reciting the words and making the gestures given in chapter 4. Call down light from infinite space above you into the cup or horn of mead, transforming the mead into pure light.

Then release the image and lift up the cup or horn of mead in both hands. Say: "Sul (or) Coel, holy goddess (or) god, receive this offering as I receive your blessing." Pour out some of the mead onto the ground or into the offering bowl. Then raise the cup or horn again and drink the remainder, letting it bring the energies of the season into you.

Sixth, sit in the west and meditate for a time on the energies of the season. Pursue the meditation for as long as you keep finding new insights. You may find it useful to take notes and meditate further on the ritual in the following days.

Seventh, dissolve the Composition of Place.

Eighth, rise from the chair and go to the west of the altar facing east. Standing there, trace the banishing Octagram of Ner in the air above the altar using the first two fingers of your right hand. Imagine your fingers drawing the octagram in a line of indigo light. Then point to the center of the octagram and say the following, vibrating the name written in capital letters:

In the sacred name (SUL or COEL) and by the holy willow, I thank the powers of Ner the Mighty, the Ninth Sphere of the Tree of Life, for hallowing and blessing this ritual of Calan Myri, and awakening for me the second station of Merlin's Wheel. Sul of the healing springs (or) Coel the master of the wild places, goddess (or) god of the Ninth Sphere, I thank you for your help in this work of self-initiation.

Ninth, perform the banishing octagram ritual of Ner.

Tenth, perform the complete closing ritual.

———— ALBAN EILIR, MARCH 21 ————

Before starting, set up your working space as a temple. The altar is at the center with an orange altar cloth. On it are three white candles in candlesticks, a bowl or cauldron of water, a bowl or cauldron of sand on which to burn incense, and the cup or horn of mead; you may also, if you wish, put on the altar any seasonal decorations suitable to the place where you live. Place a chair in the west facing the altar. Sit there for a few moments of silence to calm your mind and focus on the ritual work you are about to do, then stand up, go to the altar, and begin.

First, perform the complete opening ritual.

Second, starting at the west of the altar facing east, perform the summoning octagram ritual of Byth. Return to the altar.

Third, take your seat in the west. Then perform the Composition of Place, imagining as clearly as possible the following image as though it was physically present on the other side of the altar.

A circle of standing stones, blue-gray in color, rises from a wide plain beneath a blue sky dotted with clouds. In the center of the circle stands a brown-haired lad, Merlin the boy, who wears a cloak and trousers the same color as the stones, a tunic of unbleached linen, and leather shoes. His head is bare, and his eyes are blue and piercing. All around, just outside the circle of stones, stands a great concourse of people, the men in tunics, cloaks, and trousers, the women in cloaks and long dresses, watching him and murmuring in amazement.

Fourth, read aloud the narrative of the season in a clear, slow voice:

Merlin said to Aurelius, "If you wish a fitting monument, let the stones of the Giants' Dance in the uttermost west be brought here and set in a ring. For those stones were brought from distant places and hallowed by secret rites in the most ancient times, and each one has healing powers." This counsel seemed good to Aurelius, and he sent his brother Uther and a great host of men and Merlin to bring back the stones of the Giants' Dance.

And when they had driven off the guardians of the stones, Uther and his men tried to draw the stones from the earth to bear them back to Britain, but they could not make a single stone yield to all their efforts. Then Merlin laughed, set out such equipment as he needed, and easily drew up the stones and conveyed them to the ships, and they brought the stones back to the plain of Salisbury with great rejoicing. There, by Merlin's art, the great stones were set up in a mighty ring, and there the people of Britain made festival, and there Aurelius was crowned King of the Britons.

Fifth, rise and go to the altar. Standing at the west of the altar facing east, trace the summoning Octagram of Byth in the air above the cup or horn of mead upon the altar using the first two fingers of your right hand. Imagine your fingers drawing the octagram in a line of orange light. Then point to the center of the octagram and say the following, vibrating the name written in capital letters:

In the sacred name MABON and by the holy hazel, I call upon the powers of Byth the Eternal, the Eighth Sphere of the Tree of Life, to hallow and bless this ritual of Alban Eilir, to awaken for me the third station of Merlin's Wheel, and to consecrate to this purpose this offering of mead. Mabon, son of Modron, ever-young god of the Eighth Sphere, aid me in calling down the light that was before the worlds in this season of Alban Eilir.

Now perform the OIW Analysis, reciting the words and making the gestures given in chapter 4. Call down light from infinite space above you into the cup or horn of mead, transforming the mead into pure light.

Then release the image and lift up the cup or horn of mead in both hands. Say: "Mabon, son of Modron, receive this offering as I receive your blessing." Pour out some of the mead onto the ground or into the offering bowl. Then raise the cup or horn again and drink the remainder, letting it bring the energies of the season into you.

Sixth, sit in the west and meditate for a time on the energies of the season. Pursue the meditation for as long as you keep finding new insights. You

may find it useful to take notes and meditate further on the ritual in the following days.

Seventh, dissolve the Composition of Place.

Eighth, rise from the chair and go to the west of the altar facing east. Standing there, trace the banishing Octagram of Byth in the air above the altar using the first two fingers of your right hand. Imagine your fingers drawing the octagram in a line of orange light. Then point to the center of the octagram and say the following, vibrating the name written in capital letters:

In the sacred name MABON and by the holy hazel, I thank the powers of Byth the Eternal, the Eighth Sphere of the Tree of Life, for hallowing and blessing this ritual of Alban Eilir, and awakening for me the third station of Merlin's Wheel. Mabon, son of Modron, ever-young god of the Eighth Sphere, I thank you for your help in this work of self-initiation.

Ninth, perform the banishing octagram ritual of Byth.
Tenth, perform the complete closing ritual.

——— CALAN MAI, MAY 1 ———

Before starting, set up your working space as a temple. The altar is at the center with a green altar cloth. On it are three white candles in candlesticks, a bowl or cauldron of water, a bowl or cauldron of sand on which to burn incense, and the cup or horn of mead; you may also, if you wish, put on the altar any seasonal decorations suitable to the place where you live. Place a chair in the west facing the altar. Sit there for a few moments of silence to calm your mind and focus on the ritual work you are about to do, then stand up, go to the altar, and begin.

First, perform the complete opening ritual.

Second, starting at the west of the altar facing east, perform the summoning octagram ritual of Byw. Return to the altar.

Third, take your seat in the west. Then perform the Composition of Place, imagining as clearly as possible the following image as though it was physically present on the other side of the altar.

A narrow beach of sand stretches between a rocky shore and the rolling waves of the gray sea; the rhythmic rushing of the waves on the beach is heard, and the air is tinged with salt spray. On the shore stands a young man, Merlin the youth, wearing a tunic of unbleached linen, trousers of brown cloth, and a green cloak. His hair is brown and long, and blows in the wind. Before him stands an old woman dressed in the greens and browns and grays of earth who holds a newborn child wrapped in a crimson cloak. The woman is giving the child to Merlin. Above the shore, a castle raises its battlements against a sky at sunrise.

Fourth, read aloud the narrative of the season in a clear, slow voice:

And King Uther said to Merlin, "Give me one night of love with the lady Ygerna, and in return I will give you whatever you will ask." And Merlin replied to him, "So be it." And he changed Uther's appearance to that of Ygerna's husband the Duke of Cornwall. That night Uther rode to the castle of Tintagel and Ygerna received him lovingly, thinking he was her husband. That night was Arthur the Pendragon conceived, and that same night the Duke of Cornwall died.

When nine months had passed and Ygerna gave birth to an infant boy, Merlin went to Uther and said, "When I brought you to Ygerna you promised me whatever I would ask. I ask now for the child you begot upon her." And the king commanded the nursemaid to take the infant to Merlin, who waited beside the sea. And he took Arthur to a hidden place where he was fostered with a worthy family and did not know his birth or his heritage.

Fifth, rise and go to the altar. Standing at the west of the altar facing east, trace the summoning Octagram of Byw in the air above the cup or horn of mead upon the altar using the first two fingers of your right hand. Imagine your fingers drawing the octagram in a line of emerald-green light. Then point to the center of the octagram and say the following, vibrating the name written in capital letters:

In the sacred name ELEN and by the holy apple tree, I call upon the powers of Byw the Living, the Seventh Sphere of the Tree of Life, to hallow and bless this ritual of Calan Mai, to awaken for me the fourth station of Merlin's Wheel, and to consecrate to this purpose this offering of mead. Elen of the roads and the twilight, goddess of the Seventh Sphere, aid me in calling down the light that was before the worlds in this season of Calan Mai.

Now perform the OIW Analysis, reciting the words and making the gestures given in chapter 4. Call down light from infinite space above you into the cup or horn of mead, transforming the mead into pure light.

Then release the image and lift up the cup or horn of mead in both hands. Say: "Elen of the roads and the twilight, receive this offering as I receive your blessing." Pour out some of the mead onto the ground or into the offering bowl. Then raise the cup or horn again and drink the remainder, letting it bring the energies of the season into you.

Sixth, sit in the west and meditate for a time on the energies of the season. Pursue the meditation for as long as you keep finding new insights. You may find it useful to take notes and meditate further on the ritual in the following days.

Seventh, dissolve the Composition of Place.

Eighth, rise from the chair and go to the west of the altar facing east. Standing there, trace the banishing Octagram of Byw in the air above the altar using the first two fingers of your right hand. Imagine your fingers drawing the octagram in a line of emerald-green light. Then point to the center of the octagram and say the following, vibrating the name written in capital letters:

In the sacred name ELEN and by the holy apple tree, I thank the powers of Byw the Living, the Seventh Sphere of the Tree of Life, for hallowing and blessing this ritual of Calan Mai, and awakening for me the fourth station of Merlin's Wheel. Elen of the roads and the twilight, maiden goddess of the Tenth Sphere, I thank you for your help in this work of self-initiation.

Ninth, perform the banishing octagram ritual of Byw.

Tenth, perform the complete closing ritual.

———— ALBAΠ HEFİΠ, JUΠE 21 ————

Before starting, set up your working space as a temple. The altar is at the center with a gold altar cloth. On it are three white candles in candlesticks, a bowl or cauldron of water, a bowl or cauldron of sand on which to burn incense, and the cup or horn of mead; you may also, if you wish, put on the altar any seasonal decorations suitable to the place where you live. Place a chair in the west facing the altar. Sit there for a few moments of silence to calm your mind and focus on the ritual work you are about to do, then stand up, go to the altar, and begin.

First, perform the complete opening ritual.

Second, starting at the west of the altar facing east, perform the summoning octagram ritual of Muner. Return to the altar.

Third, take your seat in the west. Then perform the Composition of Place, imagining as clearly as possible the following image as though it was physically present on the other side of the altar.

The same circle of standing stones, blue-gray in color, stands on the plain, but now the plain is covered with flowers and the midsummer sun stands high in the heavens. In the center of the circle stands a tall figure, Merlin the young man, clad in robes of gold. His hair is brown, bound by a golden circlet, and he wears a short, brown beard. In both his hands he holds a golden crown upraised. Before him kneels a golden-haired youth in a coat of chain mail with a sword belted about his waist. The youth's head is bare. All around the circle gathers a great crowd of people of every station: great lords and ladies in robes and mantles trimmed with fur, warriors in coats of chain mail, and the common folk of the land in their brightly colored best clothing, all raising a shout of acclamation as Merlin places the crown on Arthur's head.

Fourth, read aloud the narrative of the season in a clear, slow voice:

Then Arthur once more lightly drew the sword out of the stone. But the barons said, "Who is this youth that he should reign over us?" And Merlin answered them, "This is Arthur, who is the son of Uther Pendragon. By right of blood, as also by right of drawing the sword from the stone as you have seen this day, he is to be King of the Britons." This the barons would not allow. But when word went forth that the barons still refused their homage to Arthur, the common people of the country rose up as one and said, "We will have Arthur as our king, and he who would deny him the crown, him we will slay."

So the barons knelt before Arthur and did him homage, and Merlin anointed him and placed the crown that had been his father's upon his head. And so did Arthur become King of the Britons, and long held the realm of Logres in peace.

Fifth, rise and go to the altar. Standing at the west of the altar facing east, trace the summoning Octagram of Muner in the air above the cup or horn of mead upon the altar using the first two fingers of your right hand. Imagine your fingers drawing the octagram in a line of golden light. Then point to the center of the octagram and say the following, vibrating the name written in capital letters:

In the sacred name ESUS and by the holy oak, I call upon the powers of Muner the Lord, the Sixth Sphere of the Tree of Life, to hallow and bless this ritual of Alban Hefin, to awaken for me the fifth station of Merlin's Wheel, and to consecrate to this purpose this offering of mead. Esus, chief of tree-spirits, god of the Sixth Sphere, aid me in calling down the light that was before the worlds in this season of Alban Hefin.

Now perform the OIW Analysis, reciting the words and making the gestures given in chapter 4. Call down light from infinite space above you into the cup or horn of mead, transforming the mead into pure light.

Then release the image and lift up the cup or horn of mead in both hands. Say: "Esus, chief of tree-spirits, receive this offering as I receive your blessing." Pour out some of the mead onto the ground or into the offering bowl. Then raise the cup or horn again and drink the remainder, letting it bring the energies of the season into you.

Sixth, sit in the west and meditate for a time on the energies of the season. Pursue the meditation for as long as you keep finding new insights. You

may find it useful to take notes and meditate further on the ritual in the following days.

Seventh, dissolve the Composition of Place.

Eighth, rise from the chair and go to the west of the altar facing east. Standing there, trace the banishing Octagram of Muner in the air above the altar using the first two fingers of your right hand. Imagine your fingers drawing the octagram in a line of golden light. Then point to the center of the octagram and say the following, vibrating the name written in capital letters:

In the sacred name ESUS and by the holy oak, I thank the powers of Muner the Lord, the Sixth Sphere of the Tree of Life, for hallowing and blessing this ritual of Alban Hefin, and awakening for me the fifth station of Merlin's Wheel. Esus, chief of tree-spirits, god of the Sixth Sphere, I thank you for your help in this work of self-initiation.

Ninth, perform the banishing octagram ritual of Muner.
Tenth, perform the complete closing ritual.

CALAN GWYNGALAF, AUGUST 1

Before starting, set up your working space as a temple. The altar is at the center with a red altar cloth. On it are three white candles in candlesticks, a bowl or cauldron of water, a bowl or cauldron of sand on which to burn incense, and the cup or horn of mead; you may also, if you wish, put on the altar any seasonal decorations suitable to the place where you live. Place a chair in the west facing the altar. Sit there for a few moments of silence to calm your mind and focus on the ritual work you are about to do, then stand up, go to the altar, and begin.

First, perform the complete opening ritual.

Second, starting at the west of the altar facing east, perform the summoning octagram ritual of Modur. Return to the altar.

Third, take your seat in the west. Then perform the Composition of Place, imagining as clearly as possible the following image as though it was physically present on the other side of the altar.

A great oak rises in the midst of dense forest. At the foot of the oak is an outcropping of gray stone, and from a cleft in the stone a spring bubbles up, giving birth to a narrow stream that flows away. Other trees press close all around and sunlight filtered through their leaves dapples the ground; the song of birds is everywhere, and deer, boars, and other wild things move through the forest. Beside the spring, sitting with his back to the oak, is Merlin, the man of middle years, his beard long and his brown hair unkempt. He is wrapped in a cloak the orange color of autumn leaves, and he gazes down into the waters of the spring as though he sees something there that other eyes do not see. Beside him sits a gray wolf, its tongue lolling; Merlin's hand rests on the wolf's back.

Fourth, read aloud the narrative of the season in a clear, slow voice:

Then Merlin said, "Dearer to me than the haunts of humankind is the wood, and there will I go and dwell." And he left the court of Arthur, and no one saw the manner of his leaving; and he journeyed to the forest of Caledon and to the place where the well of Galabes springs forth within a grove of great trees, and there he made his dwelling. All the wild things of that country knew him and feared him not; the deer gathered to his call, the wild boars watched their piglets play at his feet, and a wolf came from the northern moors to sit beside him and be his companion in the forest.

To him came messengers from the court of Arthur, and lastly his sister Ganieda, asking him to return, but he would not leave the wood, even as summer turned to winter. Finally there came to him Taliesin, the wisest of all the bards of Britain, who did not ask him to return, but conversed with him concerning the secrets of nature.

Fifth, rise and go to the altar. Standing at the west of the altar facing east, trace the summoning Octagram of Modur in the air above the cup or horn of mead altar using the first two fingers of your right hand. Imagine your fingers drawing the octagram in a line of red light. Then point to the center of the octagram and say the following, vibrating the name written in capital letters:

In the sacred name TARANIS and by the holy ash tree, I call upon the powers of Modur the Mover, the Fifth Sphere of the Tree of Life, to hallow and bless this ritual of Calan Gwyngalaf, to awaken for me the sixth station of Merlin's Wheel, and to consecrate to this purpose this offering of mead. Taranis of the thunders, mighty god of the Fifth Sphere, aid me in calling down the light that was before the worlds in this season of Calan Gwyngalaf.

Now perform the OIW Analysis, reciting the words and making the gestures given in chapter 4. Call down light from infinite space above you into the cup or horn of mead, transforming the mead into pure light.

Then release the image and lift up the cup or horn of mead in both hands. Say: "Taranis, mighty god, receive this offering as I receive your blessing." Pour out some of the mead onto the ground or into the offering bowl. Then raise the cup or horn again and drink the remainder, letting it bring the energies of the season into you.

Sixth, sit in the west and meditate for a time on the energies of the season. Pursue the meditation for as long as you keep finding new insights. You

may find it useful to take notes and meditate further on the ritual in the following days.

Seventh, dissolve the Composition of Place.

Eighth, rise from the chair and go to the west of the altar facing east. Standing there, trace the banishing Octagram of Modur in the air above the altar using the first two fingers of your right hand. Imagine your fingers drawing the octagram in a line of brilliant red light. Then point to the center of the octagram and say the following, vibrating the name in capital letters:

In the sacred name TARANIS and by the holy ash tree, I thank the powers of Modur the Mover, the Fifth Sphere of the Tree of Life, for hallowing and blessing this ritual of Calan Gwyngalaf, and awakening for me the sixth station of Merlin's Wheel. Taranis of the thunders, mighty god of the Fifth Sphere, I thank you for your help in this work of self-initiation.

Ninth, perform the banishing octagram ritual of Modur.

Tenth, perform the complete closing ritual.

──── ALBAꞳ ELFED, SEPTEMBER 22 ────

Before starting, set up your working space as a temple. The altar is at the center with a blue altar cloth. On it are three white candles in candlesticks, a bowl or cauldron of water, a bowl or cauldron of sand on which to burn incense, and the cup or horn of mead; you may also, if you wish, put on the altar any seasonal decorations suitable to the place where you live. Place a chair in the west facing the altar. Sit there for a few moments of silence to calm your mind and focus on the ritual work you are about to do, then stand up, go to the altar, and begin.

First, perform the complete opening ritual.

Second, starting at the west of the altar facing east, perform the summoning octagram ritual of Ener. Return to the altar.

Third, take your seat in the west. Then perform the Composition of Place, imagining as clearly as possible the following image, as though it was physically present on the other side of the altar.

A grassy shore slopes down to the sea. On the shore stand three men, and beside them a fourth lies on the grass. To the left is Taliesin, a youthful man with black hair, dressed in robes of blue, green, and white; he has a harp cradled in one arm. To the right is Bedwyr, a middle-aged man with blond hair going to gray, wearing a battered coat of chain mail, an iron helmet that does not cover his face, and leather hose; he has a sword hanging from a belt around his waist. To one side lies Arthur, wearing armor like Bedwyr's; his face is pale, his hair and beard golden, and his coat of mail is hacked and stained with blood. In the center is Merlin the old man. He wears a great cloak of crimson red and a long white robe; his arms are upraised; his hair and beard, both long, are gray. In the distance, beneath a blue autumn sky scattered with clouds, a ship with a single square sail draws near.

Fourth, read aloud the narrative of the season in a clear, slow voice:

Then Taliesin and Merlin went down among the fallen, and there found Arthur lying upon the grass, red with many wounds, and Bedwyr, the last of his warriors, kneeling beside him, all alone save Arthur and the dead. And Taliesin asked, "Does the king still live?" And Bed-wyr answered, "He does, and when he goes to his grave so shall I."

Then Merlin laughed and said, "Not wise the thought, a grave for Arthur! Be of good cheer and lift up your head, and you will behold a wonder." And Bedwyr looked, and a ship was coming toward the shore beside the field of battle. "That is the ship of Barinthus," said Merlin then, "who knows well the waters and the stars of heaven, and he shall bear Arthur to the Isle of Avalon, where Morgen the queen of that isle will heal him of his wounds. There shall he abide, king once and king to be, until he comes again."

Fifth, rise and go to the altar. Standing at the west of the altar facing east, trace the summoning Octagram of Ener in the air above the cup or horn of mead upon the altar using the first two fingers of your right hand. Imagine your fingers drawing the octagram in a line of sky-blue light. Then point to the center of the octagram and say the following, vibrating the name written in capital letters:

In the sacred name BELINUS and by the holy birch, I call upon the powers of Ener the Namer, the Fourth Sphere of the Tree of Life, to hallow and bless this ritual of Alban Elfed, to awaken for me the seventh station of Merlin's Wheel, and to consecrate to this purpose this offering of mead. Belinus, the Lord of the Year, god of the Fourth Sphere, aid me in calling down the light that was before the worlds in this season of Alban Elfed.

Now perform the OIW Analysis, reciting the words and making the gestures given in chapter 4. Call down light from infinite space above you into the cup or horn of mead, transforming the mead into pure light.

Then release the image and lift up the cup or horn of mead in both hands. Say: "Belinus, great god, receive this offering as I receive your blessing." Pour out some of the mead onto the ground or into the offering bowl. Then raise the cup or horn again and drink the remainder, letting it bring the energies of the season into you.

Sixth, sit in the west and meditate for a time on the energies of the season. Pursue the meditation for as long as you keep finding new insights. You may find it useful to take notes and meditate further on the ritual in the following days.

Seventh, dissolve the Composition of Place.

Eighth, rise from the chair and go to the west of the altar facing east. Standing there, trace the banishing Octagram of Ener in the air above the altar using the first two fingers of your right hand. Imagine your fingers drawing the octagram in a line of sky-blue light. Then point to the center of the octagram and say the following, vibrating the name written in capital letters:

> In the sacred name BELINUS and by the holy birch, I thank the powers of Ener the Namer, the Fourth Sphere of the Tree of Life, for hallowing and blessing this ritual of Alban Elfed, and awakening for me the seventh station of Merlin's Wheel. Belinus, the Lord of the Year, great god of the Fourth Sphere, I thank you for your help in this work of self-initiation.

Ninth, perform the banishing octagram ritual of Ener.

Tenth, perform the complete closing ritual.

———— CALAN TACHWEDD, NOVEMBER ————

Before starting, set up your working space as a temple. The altar is at the center with a black altar cloth. On it are three white candles in candlesticks, a bowl or cauldron of water, a bowl or cauldron of sand on which to burn incense, and the cup or horn of mead; you may also, if you wish, put on the altar any seasonal decorations suitable to the place where you live. Place a chair in the west facing the altar. Sit there for a few moments of silence to calm your mind and focus on the ritual work you are about to do, then stand up, go to the altar, and begin.

First, perform the complete opening ritual.

Second, starting at the west of the altar facing east, perform the summoning octagram ritual of Iau. Return to the altar.

Third, take your seat in the west. Then perform the Composition of Place, imagining as clearly as possible the following image as though it was physically present on the other side of the altar.

In a forest grove in autumn, tall oaks rise high above a forest floor covered with brown fallen leaves, and a few leaves still cling to the branches above. In the midst of the grove stands a newly made earthen mound with a low door that faces you, opening into utter darkness. Two tall stones flank the door, carved in spiral patterns. In front of the door stands Merlin the ancient, his hair and beard white, wearing a plain white robe. To his right stands an old woman dressed in black, her hair gray, her face resembling Merlin's. To his left stands Taliesin in his robes of green, blue, and white. Merlin extends one hand to each of them and they each hold his hand in both of theirs as they say their farewells.

Fourth, read aloud the narrative of the season in a clear, slow voice:

And when Arthur was gone Merlin returned again to the forest of Caledon and to the well of Galabes. To him came his sister Ganieda, who had been wed to one of the kings of that land and was now widowed, and she dwelt with him in the forest.

And Ganieda built for him beside the well of Galabes a chamber in which were seventy windows, so that through them he could see all the stars of heaven. And when it was done Merlin said to her and to Taliesin, "I shall now depart from among you and from all mortal beings, for it is my fate to go alive into the earth, and there remain." And he bid them farewell and went into the chamber that was prepared for him, and from there passed into the earth, nor has any mortal being seen him since that day.

Fifth, rise and go to the altar. Standing at the west of the altar facing east, trace the summoning Octagram of Iau in the air above the cup or horn of mead altar using the first two fingers of your right hand. Imagine your fingers drawing the octagram in a line of pure white light. Then point to the center of the octagram and say the following, vibrating the name written in capital letters:

In the sacred name CERIDWEN and by the holy yew, I call upon the powers of Iau the Yoke, which reflects the three highest Spheres of the Tree of Life, to hallow and bless this ritual of Calan Tachwedd, to awaken for me the last station of Merlin's Wheel, and to consecrate to this purpose this offering of mead. Ceridwen the Wise, goddess of the cauldron of Iau, aid me in calling down the light that was before the worlds in this season of Calan Tachwedd.

Now perform the OIW Analysis, reciting the words and making the gestures given in chapter 4. Call down light from infinite space above you into the cup or horn of mead, transforming the mead into pure light.

Then release the image and lift up the cup or horn of mead in both hands. Say: "Ceridwen, goddess of initiation, receive this offering as I receive your blessing." Pour out some of the mead onto the ground or into the offering bowl. Then raise the cup or horn again and drink the remainder, letting it bring the energies of the season into you.

Sixth, sit in the west and meditate for a time on the energies of the season. Pursue the meditation for as long as you keep finding new insights. You may find it useful to take notes and meditate further on the ritual in the following days.

Seventh, dissolve the Composition of Place.

Eighth, rise from the chair and go to the west of the altar facing east. Standing there, trace the banishing Octagram of Iau in the air above the altar using the first two fingers of your right hand. Imagine your fingers drawing the octagram in a line of pure white light. Then point to the center of the octagram and say the following, vibrating the name written in capital letters:

In the sacred name CERIDWEN and by the holy yew, I thank the powers of Iau the Yoke, which reflects the three highest Spheres of the Tree of Life, for hallowing and blessing this ritual of Calan Tachwedd, and awakening for me the last station of Merlin's Wheel. Ceridwen the Wise, goddess of the cauldron of Iau, I thank you for your help in this work of self-initiation.

Ninth, perform the banishing octagram ritual of Iau.
Tenth, perform the complete closing ritual.

CHAPTER EIGHT

DANCING ROUND MERLIN'S WHEEL

The eight rituals of Merlin's Wheel can be worked entirely by themselves as a system of personal initiation with nothing added to them. For those who want to go further, though, additional studies, practices, and activities can be combined with the rituals as given in this book. The rituals of Merlin's Wheel can also be practiced together by more than one person. Finally, for those who feel themselves called to the hard but rewarding labor of training in ceremonial magic, in addition to the rituals of self-initiation taught in these pages, it's entirely possible to practice the mysteries of Merlin's Wheel and the additional practices that go with them alongside the course of training and initiation in Druidical magic set out in my book *The Celtic Golden Dawn*. The pages that follow will explain how each of these things can be done.

LEARNING MORE ABOUT MERLIN

One simple and straightforward way to make the experience of self-initiation richer and more meaningful is to explore the legends from which the rituals of Merlin's Wheel draw their symbolism. As discussed earlier in this book, Merlin has been turned into a pop culture icon over the last few centuries, and in the usual way of such things, most of the depth, strangeness, and power that once gathered around the archaic Celtic god Moridunos, He of the Sea-Fortress, has been replaced by an assortment of glossy clichés having more to do with today's cultural fashions and crowd psychology than anything else. The more effectively you are able to get past the modern veneer of pop culture to the real Merlin—ancient Celtic god, Dark Age prophet, mythic figure at the heart of an archaic mystery tradition—the more power the initiations of Merlin's Wheel will have for you.

Fortunately, there are several good modern books that can help bridge the gap. The best currently available introduction to the Merlin legend and its implications is Nikolai Tolstoy's *The Quest for Merlin*, which starts with Geoffrey of Monmouth and goes from there to put the Dark Age figures of Merlin Ambrosius and Merlin Caledonius in their historical context.

On a deeper and more magical level, R. J. Stewart's *The Prophetic Vision of Merlin* and *The Mystic Life of Merlin* (now available in a single volume titled, appropriately enough, *Merlin*) explore Geoffrey of Monmouth's two Merlin narratives, the Merlin passages in *The History of the Kings of Britain* and *The Life of Merlin*, with a keen eye for the many mystical, occult, and psychological meanings concealed in these enigmatic texts. Stewart has written and edited a number of other books about Merlin and his legends, and also helped produce a tarot deck based on the symbolism woven into the Merlin legend. While these are based on a different magical system than the one used in this book and go in directions that differ from those explored here, they are worth studying in their own right.

Some readers, especially those who are already familiar with the Western occult tradition, will also find much of value in two works by contemporary occultist Gareth Knight. *The Secret Tradition in Arthurian Legend* is a detailed analysis of the entire legend of Arthur from the standpoint of one system of Western occultism, the system created by the influential British occult author and teacher Dion Fortune. Knight has also edited a collection of Fortune's own writings on Arthurian matters, together with those of several more recent writers in the same tradition, under the title *The Arthurian Formula*. Both are well worth reading.

All these are excellent starting places. From there, the journey leads straight to the medieval Merlin narratives themselves. Nearly all of these are found embedded in the legends of King Arthur; fortunately the vogue for all things Arthurian in recent decades means that most of the traditional accounts of Merlin are readily available. Geoffrey of Monmouth's *The History of the Kings of Britain* is in print as I write this, translated into English and available in an inexpensive paperback edition. Sir Thomas Malory's *Le Morte d'Arthur*, in which Merlin features at length, has not been out of print for something like two and a half centuries. Other medieval versions of the Merlin legend are less readily available, but a little searching in used bookstores, online or off, will very often turn up treasures.

The literature of the Middle Ages takes some getting used to if you haven't read any of it before. Medieval stories were written to be read aloud—one of the most common ways to pass the time in those days was to have someone read aloud from a book while the other members of the household busied themselves with handicrafts or relaxed in the warmth from the glowing hearth. A story meant to be read aloud needs a different sense of pace and rhythm than a story meant to be read silently by one person alone. (Try reading a passage from a medieval Arthurian tale aloud sometime, imagining that you are a squire or lady-in-waiting in a noble household and the other members of the household are listening to you; you'll find that the habits of medieval authors make much more sense once you've done that.)

The reason it's worth making the effort to read medieval stories about Merlin, rather than just relying on modern versions of the legends, is that nearly all the modern versions have been watered down to an embarrassing degree. Popular fiction nowadays, even when it's supposedly set in some distant time or in a world of pure imagination, stocks its stories with characters who are basically modern people with modern interests and concerns. That helps us place ourselves in the characters' shoes and share their adventures and experiences, and thus makes the story more enjoyable for most readers, but much is lost in the process: above all, the genuine power and strangeness of distant times. The past is a foreign country. They do things differently there, and even in the medium of fiction, flattening out the past into a rehash of the present is one of the ways we make the world duller and less vivid than it would otherwise be.

Of all the reams of modern fiction written about Merlin, I know of only two novels in the English language featuring him that capture some of the archaic mystery that once gathered around He of the Sea-Fortress: *That Hideous Strength* by C. S. Lewis and *Porius: A Romance of the Dark Ages* by John Cowper Powys. Lewis, though mostly famous today as the author of *The Chronicles of Narnia* and a friend of iconic fantasy author J. R. R. Tolkien, spent his career as a professor of medieval and Renaissance literature, and understood the culture and worldview of the Middle Ages more deeply than any other scholar of his generation. The Merlin of his novel is truly medieval, a figure Geoffrey of Monmouth or Sir Thomas Malory would have recognized.

John Cowper Powys's Merlin is a stranger and mightier figure still. Powys's friends called him "the Old Earth Man," and for good reason; Powys saturated himself in the traditional folklore of the British landscape and drew from it the raw material for two novels and a great deal of vivid poetry. The Merlin of *Porius* is a wild woodland figure, somewhere on the misty borderland that connects human beings with animals and with gods, and his magic has a degree of authenticity to it worlds away from the glossy Hollywood special-effects foolery so heavily featured in pop culture these days. My guess, though it's only a guess, is that the version of Merlin presented in Powys's novel is as close as we will ever get to the primal Celtic god once worshiped on the hilltops of southern Wales and the slopes of Hart Fell.

CELEBRATIONS OF THE SEASONS

The rituals of Merlin's Wheel can also be practiced alongside some more general pattern of seasonal celebrations linked to the eight festivals of the modern Pagan year-wheel. If you already follow a Pagan spiritual path, odds are that the tradition you follow already sets out a sequence of rituals or other practices to be done at the eight stations of the year. The same is true of many varieties of alternative religion that don't identify with the word "Pagan"; most Druids and many Heathens, for example, celebrate the same eight festivals as their Pagan friends and neighbors, though of course the celebrations take very different forms.

There are a great many books in print just now that explore meditations, practices, and household activities relating to the cycle of the year and its eight stations, and much of the material these books present can be woven into the practices in this book with good effect. Almost anything that brings you into contact with the cycles of nature will help feed the subtle linkage between myth, ritual, and seasonal cycle that gives the mysteries of Merlin's Wheel their effect. The simple habit of spending some time out of doors at least once a week around the cycle of the year, quieting the mind and simply attending to what nature is doing, is an effective way of accomplishing this goal. Plenty of books that discuss Pagan spirituality from one or another perspective have other methods to offer that help to do the same thing.

On the other hand, I don't recommend trying to mash together the rituals of Merlin's Wheel with those of any other traditional set of rites celebrating the stations of the year. The rituals set out in this book have been crafted carefully to accomplish the work of self-initiation and, for that purpose, to have certain specific effects on the practitioner. Those effects may well not be compatible with the effects some other ritual is meant to produce; the result of mixing up rituals is too often rather like what happened to the inexperienced cook who wanted to bake a cake, found that the sugar jar was empty, and decided that two cups of salt would be a good substitute for two cups of sugar! Instead of trying to blend unrelated rituals together, it's normally best to participate in the ritual of your existing tradition without alteration, then, a day before or a day after, set aside the necessary time to perform the appropriate ritual from this book.

Even so, there is one form of celebration almost universal in ancient Pagan cultures that can easily be combined with the ceremonies of Merlin's Wheel. This is the sacred feast. Depending on your circumstances and preferences, this can be as simple as ordering an especially fancy pizza on the nights when you perform the rituals in this book, or as complex as helping to cook and serve an elaborate dinner for your family, friends, or fellow practitioners of these mysteries.

Whatever kind of feast fits your schedule, your pocketbook, and your taste, one thing should always be included: an offering of part of the food to the deity who presides over the seasonal ritual. This is what transforms an ordinary meal into a spiritually powerful action. Simply take a portion of the main dish—a slice of the fancy pizza, if that's what's on the menu that evening—put it on a plate of its own, and set it on something that's higher than the level of the table from which you'll be eating. As you set the offering in the place you've chosen, say, "[*Name of deity*], please accept this offering and join us in this celebration." You can use some more ornate ritual of offering if you follow a tradition that includes one, but something this simple is entirely sufficient.

Then, when you've finished your meal, take the offering down and set it on the table from which you've eaten your share of the food. You (and everyone else present, if you have guests) should then eat the offering in silence.[58] When it's gone, say, "[*Name of deity*], thank you for your bounty and your blessing." Again, you can use some more complicated prayer of thanks if you wish or if the tradition you follow provides one, but a few simple words of thanks are all that's necessary.

It's worth taking a moment here to explain the point of this little rite because too many people these days tend to confuse the traditional Pagan concept of making offerings to the gods with the Christian concept of sacrifice, with all its attendant baggage of self-denial and poorly camouflaged masochism. You don't make offerings to the gods because you think you've been bad or because you think that depriving yourself of something you like will make the gods happy. (It won't.) You make offerings to the gods in precisely the same spirit that you might offer a visiting friend a cold beer or a seat at the dinner table.[59]

To the ancient Pagan way of thinking, while there's an important difference between gods and human beings, it's not the absolute distinction as the monotheist faiths generally insist on. The gods are wise, strong, and generous to a quite literally superhuman degree, but the relationships between gods and human beings are more a matter of fellowship and community than cringing subservience. You offer a portion of your feast to the god or goddess who presides over the station of the year-wheel to welcome his or her presence. The god or goddess receives the gift and returns it, blessed with his or her spiritual power, and you partake gratefully of the food that he or she has

---

58. It's probably necessary to note that in modern Wicca, food offerings made to deities aren't consumed by the worshipers, and some people of that faith overgeneralize from that habit to insist that no one should ever do so. That's news to Hindus, who reverently eat *prasad* (food offered to divinities) as members of their faith have done for thousands of years, and to practitioners of Shinto, who sip rice wine that has been offered to the *kami* every time they visit a shrine. Most other polytheist faiths, ancient and modern, do some equivalent of the same thing. It's wholly appropriate for Wiccans to practice their faith and deal with food offerings as they see fit, of course, but the mysteries of Merlin's Wheel are not Wiccan ceremonies and needn't follow Wiccan rules.

59. I have discussed this way of thinking about offerings at some length in my book *A World Full of Gods*.

blessed in acknowledgment of the abundant gifts that the gods shower on humanity and the living earth.

Group Workings

The rituals in this book have been designed for aspirants to the mysteries who work the rites of Merlin's Wheel alone. Given the diversity of the modern Pagan and magical scenes, that's necessary—most of the people who purchase this book and set out to practice its rites won't have access to anyone else interested in working the mysteries along with them. As we've seen, it also reflects the role of self-initiation in the mystery traditions of late classical antiquity, and in the long years of hiding since open celebration of the mysteries was suppressed by force.

Nonetheless, if the response to my previous books on Celtic spirituality and Druid magic is anything to go by, there will be some readers who want to perform the rituals in this book together with other people. That's an option for those who wish to pursue it. Since the groups in question will more than likely cover the entire range of numbers from two people to several dozen, and the level of previous magical experience among the participants may range from complete novices to capable operative mages with decades of practice under their ceremonial belts, detailed scripts and instructions would be a waste of time. Certain basic principles, however, can be reviewed here.

The first principle is that the mysteries of Merlin's Wheel are not intended to be a spectator sport. As far as possible, every participant should take some role in the ceremony. It requires very little training in ritual performance to purify the space with water, to consecrate it with fire, or to read aloud the narrative of the season. It requires very little more to perform the Lesser Ritual of the Pentagram or to perform some other more complex part of the ritual work.

The kind of esoteric grandstanding in which a single more experienced person does all the ritual work while everyone else is assigned the role of admiring audience is embarrassingly common in some corners of the Pagan and magical communities these days and should be avoided. The more demanding parts in the ritual can certainly be assigned to more experienced participants, at least at first, but part of the goal of any group magical working should be to help all the participants get to a level of experience and skill that will allow any of them to handle any part successfully. One of the initiatory dimensions of the mysteries of Merlin's Wheel is precisely that it teaches the practitioner to perform an effective set of magical workings; that same dimension is as important in group work as in solitary self-initiation.

That said, there's a flip side to the point just made. Not everyone who wants to get involved in a ceremony of this kind will necessarily be willing to invest the necessary time to learn and practice a part, or the effort needed to do it well. You owe it to yourself, and to the other participants in the ceremony, to reserve the roles that take work for those who are prepared to do the work in question, and to assign those who don't have the time or the willingness to prepare for the ritual to less important parts, or to the sidelines.

It also happens from time to time that someone gets involved in a ritual working of this kind with the intention, conscious or otherwise, of disrupting it. Many people these days have unresolved feelings of personal inadequacy and rebelliousness, and some of them vent those feelings by taking an adversarial role in any group setting. Those of my readers who have been involved in any part of the alternative-spirituality scene have likely seen this pattern of behavior in action far too often for their comfort. If you have such a person in a group that's enacting the mysteries of Merlin's Wheel and a friendly conversation or two with the person doesn't result in any change in behavior, it really is the best option either to remove that person from the group, if that's an option, or to walk away. Nothing will be gained by trying to placate a person whose interest in the group is limited to how much disruption he or she can cause and how quickly the group can be wrecked or hijacked for some unrelated purpose.

The second principle is that practice makes perfect. Just as you need to practice each of the elements of the ceremony beforehand if you're working the rites of Merlin's Wheel alone, if you're doing the ritual with others, your group needs to meet at least once and go through the complete ceremony before celebrating each station of the Wheel. This is true even when the group has been meeting and celebrating the rituals for years. Inevitably people will rotate into new ritual roles, experienced participants will forget how things worked a year before, and so on. Regular practice is the one way to keep this sort of thing from messing up your ceremony—and of course this means solitary practice, for those who have significant ritual work to do, as well as group practice for all.

A great many people in today's alternative-spirituality scene like to focus on spontaneous, improvisational ceremonies. That's fine, but it limits the kind of ceremony you can perform to those that can be done by untrained participants without practice and preparation. The ceremonies of Merlin's Wheel don't fall into that category. To borrow a metaphor from music, there are pieces of music that are suited to community sing-alongs and there are pieces of music for which you need capable musicians willing to put in hours of practice, and restricting things to the community sing-along level means that there's plenty of really good music that will never be performed. The ceremonies of Merlin's Wheel aren't all the way over to the end of the spectrum occupied by Bach and Mozart, to be sure, but they aren't the kind of thing you can just pick up and start singing out of the book. Invest a little time in study, practice, and preparation, and the results will more than repay your efforts.

A group of people working together can also include other activities alongside practice and the celebration of the mysteries. There's much to be said, for example, for setting up an informal book club for members of the group that want to study the Merlin legends together, and at least as much to be said for having a feast together after each celebration. Other seasonal activities can just as easily be added to the schedule depending on the time and resources available to group members.

The final principle I want to cover here is that group workings may be enjoyable (or may not be!), but they aren't required. If you can't find anyone else who wants to perform the ceremonies with you; if you simply would rather skip the drama and follow a solitary path; if you get involved in a group and it turns out, for one reason or another, to be more trouble than it's worth— you can always do things entirely on your own. You don't need anyone else's help or approval to follow the path of self-initiation into the mysteries of Merlin's Wheel. When you bought your copy of this book it came with all the permission you need to work the rituals it contains. Now all you have to do is study, practice, and perform the ceremonies, by yourself or with others, with or without the additional studies or activities mentioned in this chapter, in as simple or as ornate a form as you happen to prefer.

†HE MYSTERIES OF MERLIN
AND †HE CELTIC GOLDEN DAWN

One additional choice before you is whether you want to make your celebrations of the ceremonies of *The Mysteries of Merlin* part of the broader process of magical study and training outlined in my book *The Celtic Golden Dawn*. As mentioned in the chapters you've already read, the rituals of *The Mysteries of Merlin* rely on the system of Druidical magic taught in that earlier book. You don't have to take on the labor of becoming an initiate of that system in order to benefit from the rites of self-initiation covered here. On the other hand, the material covered in each book is completely compatible with the other, and the two bodies of lore fuse together neatly to yield an even more effective system of magical self-initiation than either one provides on its own.

You'll want to make a few minor adjustments if you're celebrating the rituals in this book alongside the course of training given in *The Celtic Golden Dawn*. The opening and closing rituals in this book are simplified versions of the ones given in the earlier book, and the more complete versions from *The Celtic Golden Dawn* should be used instead. You should also have the cross and circle on your altar, in the position appropriate to the grade you're working, and wear your white robe with the sash or sashes of any grades you have earned. Finally, once you have made and consecrated your wand and serpent's egg, you may certainly use these in the Druid Circle ceremonies of *The Mysteries of Merlin*.

The rituals of the octagram presented in the Druid Circle of this book are not included in *The Celtic Golden Dawn*, but they can readily be incorporated into the rituals and practices of the Druid Grade of that book. They provide an effective way to summon and banish the energies of the spheres of the Tree of Life and may be used in place of the Supreme Ritual of the Pentagram in ceremonies of the Druid Grade.

A few words about meshing the grades and the circles may also be helpful. The system of training presented in *The Celtic Golden Dawn* assigns a minimum of four months preparation before the Ovate Grade initiation, a minimum of eight months before the Bardic Grade initiation, and a minimum of a year before the Druid Grade initiation. If you start work on *The Celtic Golden Dawn* and *The Mysteries of Merlin* at the same time, and complete the work of each grade in the minimum time allotted for it, the Ovate

Circle will occupy the year you spend as an Aspirant and Ovate, the Bardic Circle the year you spend as a Bard, and thereafter, as a Druid, you may celebrate the ceremonies of the Druid Circle.

If it takes you longer than the minimum to complete the training of the grades, the choice is yours whether to advance to the next circle at the completion of the year or to hold off until you're ready to take the initiation of the corresponding grade. The latter, while it requires a certain amount of patience, is worth considering. In magical training, there are no prizes for hurrying through the work—quite the contrary, those who succeed best are those who take their time and are sure they have mastered one stage before proceeding to the next. Those who approach the mysteries of Merlin's Wheel in that spirit will not be disappointed in the results.

OTHER MYSTERIES, OTHER GODS

I n the preceding pages I have attempted to show how the old mysteries of
Moridunos, He of the Sea-Fortress, the archaic Celtic god whose myths
come down to us in fragmentary and distorted form in the legends of Merlin,
can be revived as a system of individual practice suited for the needs of spiritual seekers in today's world. I have worked the rituals presented here and
believe that they will be as potent a tool of self-initiation for others as they
have been for me. That said, even in their heyday in late Roman times, the
mysteries of Moridunos were far from the only mysteries being celebrated in
Britain, much less the rest of the Roman world—and there is no reason why
the mysteries of Merlin's Wheel should be the only rites of their kind to be
practiced in our time.

The same process of revival and reworking I have applied to the legends
of Merlin can, in fact, be applied to any suitable body of myth or legend to
create a system of seasonal mysteries suited to regular performance by individuals and groups. Whatever deities or sacred figures you revere, whatever
tradition of spirituality and magic you happen to practice, you can craft a set
of mystery rituals suited to your own needs. If you're prepared to put in the
necessary work, the following steps will bring you to that goal.

CHOOSING A NARRATIVE

The first thing you need to do in order to craft a set of mystery rituals is to
choose the story at the core of your mysteries. As discussed earlier in this

book, the ancient mysteries seem to have started out as seasonal reenactments of stories about the gods and goddesses, and the same narrative focus
remained central to the mysteries all through their long history. The same
rule applies here: your mysteries will be telling a story, and so the very first
thing you need to do is to choose the story they will tell.

If your spiritual path is rooted in one of the well-documented polytheist
religions of Pagan antiquity, and you don't already have a story in mind, your
biggest challenge will be deciding among too many options! Whether you revere the Heathen gods of the north, the gods of Greece and Rome, the Celtic
deities of Ireland, or one of the many other options, you have a vast number
of narratives to choose from. Pick up a good collection of the myths of your
tradition, if you don't already have one somewhere on your bookshelves, and
read it from cover to cover. There are no prizes for hurrying through the process, so take your time, think about how each of the myths you read might
work as the foundation for ceremonies, then make your choice.

What if you don't happen to practice a spirituality based on one of the old
polytheist faiths? You still have plenty of options. If you work with one of the
systems of Western occultism that don't invoke Pagan deities, for example,
you still have no shortage of sacred narratives to choose from. To begin with,
the revival of the old Christian mysteries in something more closely reflect-
ing their original form—a way of initiation for those who choose to embrace
it, rather than an intolerant ideology of social and political control—is something already being explored by a range of individuals and traditions in the
independent sacramental movement within Christianity,[60] and arguably de-
serves more attention than it's received so far.

Nor are specifically religious myths the only options worth exploring as
a source for mystery rituals. Not all the mysteries of ancient times celebrated
the doings of gods—there were also local mysteries in many corners of
Greece that recounted the doings of human beings whose great deeds earned
them sacred power—and similar stories in occult tradition can readily be
used as the basis for mysteries.

Thus, for example, it would be easy and also rewarding to construct a set
of mysteries around the legendary life of Christian Rosenkreutz, the founder

---

60. See Plummer, *The Many Paths of the Independent Sacramental Movement*, for an able
    survey of some of these.

of the Rosicrucian Order. Christian Rosenkreutz and Merlin are parallel figures in many ways, as noted earlier in this book, and the same general structure set out in this book could be applied to the life of "our Father C.R.C.," as he is called in Rosicrucian writings, to produce a compelling and spiritually effective set of mysteries. A cycle of mystery workings based on the legendary figure of Hermes Trismegistus, the founder of the Hermetic tradition, would be just as easy to construct and, I suspect, just as rewarding to practice.

Another set of options, which would be particularly easy to follow using the rituals and practices in this book as a template, unfold from other aspects of the immense body of Arthurian legend from which I extracted the tale of Merlin. Modern initiatory traditions have been using Arthurian themes as the basis for their rituals since not long after the public celebration of mystery initiations became possible again. Some very impressive work has already been done along these lines, notably by British occultists in the tradition set into motion by Dion Fortune. Those readers who are interested in creating new initiations along the same lines might find it useful to study Gareth Knight's *The Secret Tradition in Arthurian Legend* and John and Caitlin Matthews' *Arthurian Magic* as starting points, and proceed from there to the original medieval sources. The abundance of narrative resources in the old Arthurian tales is such that there's very nearly no limit to the number of initiatory systems that could be developed from them.

One option that probably needs to be addressed here is the use of modern popular media as the basis for mystery workings. It's true that novels, movies, and television shows fill some of the roles today that mythology filled in the distant past, and many people have strong emotional connections to the characters of this or that popular book, film, or program. The difficulty here, of course, is that these books, films, and programs were by and large created purely for the sake of entertainment, with no noticeable spiritual content at all, and a ceremonial based on one of them will most likely initiate you into nothing more esoteric than the mysteries of twenty-first century pop culture —a tradition in which most of us are already *epoptai*!

One of the driving forces behind the revival of traditional Pagan spirituality in modern times has been the desire, strongly felt by many people, to break out of pop culture's echo chamber and engage life in a more meaningful way. The old Pagan cultures had their own problems, to be sure, but they never managed our modern state of helpless detachment from the earthy and vitalizing realities of existence. One of the great advantages of working with ancient myths and legends in a ceremonial setting is that it helps to build a bridge between our modern consciousness and the very different consciousness of the old Pagan cultures—a bridge which potentially makes it possible to fuse the best of both worlds.

Two other factors are worth keeping in mind as you choose your narrative. First of all, the ancient mysteries, since they were normally celebrated only once each year, focused on a single incident. The mysteries of Artemis at Ephesus celebrated a birth; the mysteries of Attis mourned a sacrificial death; the mysteries of Isis, like those celebrated at Eleusis, reenacted a search and recovery, and so on. In order to work your mysteries at the eight stations of the year, by contrast, you'll find it more useful to choose a sacred narrative with many important incidents so you have plenty of raw material. As you assess myths and legends for their suitability for a mystery working, spend some time thinking about how you would assign the important events in the myth to eight ceremonies.[61]

The relationship between the mythic narratives of your tradition and the cycle of the seasons is the second point that benefits from careful attention. On the one hand, some myths and legends won't fit the seasonal cycle no matter how much stretching and lopping you do; on the other, nothing restricts your choice of narrative to those that have an obvious link to the seasonal cycle. In the arrangement of the legends of Merlin presented in this book, the life of Merlin functions as a metaphor for the cycle of the year, in a pattern much used in ancient Pagan traditions; elements of standard myth such as the birth of the miraculous child at midwinter, and bits of historical fact such as the orientation of Stonehenge to the midsummer sunrise, made it easy to fit the legend to the calendar in ways that are sometimes obvious and sometimes subtle. (Most of these have been left for initiates of the mysteries of Merlin's Wheel to tease out in their meditations.)

---

61. The same is true if you have some other sacred calendar in mind for your mysteries. The discussion here will assume you're using the eightfold wheel of the year; make the appropriate adjustments if you want to arrange your mysteries according to a different annual pattern.

That's one way that you can fit a narrative to a seasonal cycle. There are others, of course. Always keep in mind that the cycle of the year isn't the same from place to place. Not everyone lives in a region where the seasons follow the sort of generic, temperate, northwestern-European pattern that's standard in many modern Pagan traditions. If your seasonal markers are different—if you live in an arid region where the autumn rains mark the beginning of the season of life and vegetative growth, for example, or a semi-tropical region where the flowers bloom year round and other indications track the seasonal changes—consider fitting your narrative to the year-wheel you actually experience rather than feeling bound to established patterns irrelevant to the environment in which you actually live.

Choosing a Magical System

In order to transform your chosen narrative into the basis for a cycle of mystery rituals for the purpose of self-initiation, you'll need to have a sufficiently rich language of ritual to open a sacred space and invoke the energies corresponding to the eight stages of the narrative and the eight seasons of the year. The rituals of Merlin's Wheel met that need by drawing on the system of Druidical ceremonial magic I created for my book *The Celtic Golden Dawn*. Ceremonial magic of one kind or another is a valid option for those who find it appealing, but it's not the only option available to those who want to enter the path of the mysteries.

Two factors should be kept in mind here. First, ceremonial magic is not for everyone, nor should it be. If you already practice some other kind of magic, or a spiritual tradition that includes a suitable set of rituals, there's no reason not to use that, so long as the tradition itself doesn't forbid such adaptations. In the Order of Bards Ovates and Druids (OBOD) and the Ancient Order of Druids in America (AODA), for example, ceremonial magic plays no part in their study programs, but the rituals that both orders use for opening and closing a grove and coming into contact with spiritual powers are entirely adequate for mystery workings. (I am an initiate of both these orders and have experimented with the ceremonies of Merlin's Wheel using both sets of ritual methods with excellent results.) Though I have no personal experience with their methods, there's every reason to think that modern eclectic Wicca, the various schools of British Traditional Witchcraft, and other Pagan, Heathen, and polytheist traditions have suitably robust and effective ritual methods for the purpose of working mystery ceremonies of the kind explored in this book.

This brings us to the second factor I have in mind, which is that no magical system is suited to every pantheon or traditional myth, nor is any pantheon or myth suited to every magical system. It used to be very common for initiates of the Hermetic Order of the Golden Dawn and its offshoots to insist that all gods and myths could be plugged into their symbolic system without distortion, and such monuments of misguided scholarship as Aleister Crowley's *777* attempted to lop and stretch all the world's pantheons and systems of spiritual thought until they fit into the Procrustean bed of the Golden Dawn's symbolism.

There are other options. One of them is to rework the Golden Dawn system itself, using the robust Golden Dawn magical methods with a different symbolic structure, drawn from the tradition you wish to use. That was the approach I took in *The Celtic Golden Dawn*, and the testimony I've received from several hundred people who have worked with the methods in that book suggests that it's a viable approach. Since it derives its symbolism and spiritual dimensions from the eighteenth- and nineteenth-century Druid Revival traditions, however, the system of *The Celtic Golden Dawn* is suited only for working with deities and mythic narratives relevant to those traditions—basically, those that draw their inspiration from the folklore and legends of Wales, Cornwall, and Brittany, the three Brythonic Celtic cultures, from their ancestors in ancient Britain and Gaul, or from their echoes in Arthurian legend.[62]

What if you want to use ceremonial magic but prefer not to work with either the Judeo-Christian symbolism of the Hermetic Order of the Golden Dawn or the Druid Revival symbolism of *The Celtic Golden Dawn*? At the moment, your options are somewhat limited, unless you're prepared to devote the necessary time to study the Golden Dawn or some other system of ceremonial magic and then rework it to fit your preferred pantheon and tradition. A book edited by the irrepressible Lon Milo DuQuette, *Llewellyn's*

---

62. The languages and cultures of Ireland, Scotland, and the Isle of Man derive from the other side of the Celtic cultural matrix, the Goidelic side, and their traditions differ sharply from those of the Brythonic Celts—sharply enough that the system presented in *The Celtic Golden Dawn* cannot be used with material from the Goidelic cultures without a complete reworking.

Complete Book of Ceremonial Magick: A Comprehensive Guide to the Western Mystery Tradition, includes a chapter by me explaining in detail how to convert basic Golden Dawn magical techniques for use with any of the traditional polytheist faiths of the Western world. I am planning a full-length book on the same subject. Until that sees print, though, you may need to settle for something simpler.

Wriᴛiɴɢ, Rᴇwriᴛiɴɢ, aɴᴅ Exᴘᴇriмᴇɴᴛaᴛioɴ

Once you've chosen your tradition, your narrative, and your magical system, all that remains is putting these things together into a set of mystery ceremonies keyed to the eight stations of the year. If you like, you can use the ceremonies of *The Mysteries of Merlin* as templates, or you can do something entirely different. Just as the mysteries of Eleusis, Agrai, and Andania used different rituals to celebrate the mysteries of Demeter and Persephone, you can celebrate your mysteries in whatever way works for you. In the mysteries, as in the broader Pagan traditions from which they derived, there's no such thing as "one true way."

The work before you is simply to write out a set of rituals and then perform them and see how well they work. Your first drafts may be fairly clunky. (Mine usually are.) Reading the rituals aloud several times in private, and listening to the way the words flow, is one way to help them get past the clunky stage. Still, the only test that ultimately matters is the test of practice.

Magic, according to the definition made famous by the great English occultist Dion Fortune, is the art and science of causing change in consciousness according to will. As an art, it's a performing art, even though the performer and the audience are the same person. As a science, it's an experimental science, even though the scientist, the experimental subject, and the laboratory in which the experiment takes place are all, once again, the same person. What this implies is that it's helpful to approach magical ritual the way you would approach playing a piece of music, say, or carrying out a scientific experiment. It's not something you do once and for all; it's a learning process in which you and the framework of the process (the melody, the experimental design, or in this case, the text of the ceremony) adapt to each other. As you gain experience and skill, you'll change the way you approach the ceremony, but you may also find that changes to the ritual text are called for.

Take your time, try various options, and see which ones work best for you. Remember that nothing is set in stone and that the mysteries celebrated at Eleusis all those centuries ago—or, for that matter, those celebrated on Bryn Myrddin near Carmarthen and Hart Fell in the Scottish Lowlands—were the result of exactly such a process of experimentation and adaptation. As you celebrate the mysteries, whether you choose the mysteries of Merlin set out in this book or a set of ceremonies you create yourself, you are participating in one of the great spiritual transformations of history: the rebirth of Pagan spirituality after more than sixteen centuries of violent suppression and persecution. The hard work and flexibility needed to make the mysteries you celebrate as rich and rewarding as they can be is a fitting contribution to that project.

Bibliography

Aneirin. *Y Gododdin*. Translated by Steve Short. Burnham-on-Sea, UK: Llanerch Press, 1994.

Blacker, Carmen. *The Catalpa Bow: A Study of Shamanistic Practices in Japan*. London: Allen and Unwin, 1986.

Burkert, Walter. *Greek Religion*. Translated by John Raffan. Cambridge, MA: Harvard University Press, 1985.

Conlee, John, ed. *Prose Merlin*. Kalamazoo, MI: Medieval Institute Publications, 1998.

Crowley, Aleister. *777 and Other Qabalistic Writings of Aleister Crowley*. York Beach, ME: Weiser Books, 1973.

Crowley, John. *Aegypt*. New York: Bantam Books, 1987.

DuQuette, Lon Milo, ed. *Llewellyn's Complete Book of Ceremonial Magick: A Comprehensive Guide to the Western Mystery Tradition*. Woodbury, MN: Llewellyn Publications, 2020.

Fortune, Dion. *The Cosmic Doctrine*. Cheltenham, UK: Helios Book Service, 1966.

Gantz, Jeffrey, trans. *The Mabinogion*. London: Penguin, 1976.

Geoffrey of Monmouth. *The History of the Kings of Britain*. Translated by Lewis Thorpe. London: Penguin, 1966.

Geoffrey of Monmouth. *The Vita Merlini* [The Life of Merlin]. Translated by John Jay Parry. Urbana, IL: University of Illinois Press, 1925.

Gerald of Wales. *The Journey Through Wales and The Description of Wales.* Translated by Lewis Thorpe. London: Penguin, 1978.

Green, Miranda J. *The Gods of Roman Britain.* Aylesbury, UK: Shire Publications, 1983.

Greer, John Michael. *The Celtic Golden Dawn: An Original & Complete Curriculum of Druidical Study.* Woodbury, MN: Llewellyn Publications, 2013.

———. *The Coelbren Alphabet: The Forgotten Oracle of the Welsh Bards.* Woodbury, MN: Llewellyn Publications, 2017.

———. *Monsters: An Investigator's Guide to Magical Beings.* St. Paul, MN: Llewellyn Publications, 2001.

———. *Mystery Teachings from the Living Earth.* San Francisco, CA: Red Wheel Weiser, 2012.

——— and Christopher Warnock, trans. *Picatrix: The Classic Medieval Handbook of Astrological Magic.* Iowa City, IA: Adocentyn Press, 2010.

———. *A World Full of Gods: An Inquiry into Polytheism.* Tucson, AZ: ADF Publications, 2005.

Hawkins, Gerald S. *Stonehenge Decoded.* New York: Dell, 1965.

Knight, Gareth, Dion Fortune, and Margaret Lumley-Brown. *The Arthurian Formula.* Loughborough, UK: Thoth, 2006.

Knight, Gareth, ed. *Dion Fortune's Rites of Isis and of Pan.* Cheltenham, UK: Skylight Press, 2013.

———. *The Secret Tradition in Arthurian Legend.* Wellingborough, UK: Aquarian, 1983.

Lewis, C. S. *That Hideous Strength.* London: Bodley Head, 1945.

Matthews, John, and Caitlin Matthews. *Arthurian Magic: A Practical Guide to the Wisdom of Camelot.* Woodbury, MN: Llewellyn Publications, 2017.

Meyer, Marvin W., ed. *The Ancient Mysteries: A Sourcebook of Sacred Texts.* Philadelphia: University of Pennsylvania Press, 1987.

Morris, John. *The Age of Arthur: A History of the British Isles from 350 to 650.* New York: Charles Scribner's Sons, 1973.

Nichols, Ross, and James Kirkup. *The Cosmic Shape.* London: Forge, 1946.

Parke, H.W. *Festivals of the Athenians*. Ithaca, NY: Cornell University Press, 1977.

Pausanias. *Guide to Greece*, two vols. Translated by Peter Levi. London: Penguin, 1971.

Plummer, John P. *The Many Paths of the Independent Sacramental Movement*. Berkeley, CA: Apocryphile, 2006.

Powys, John Cowper. *Porius: A Romance of the Dark Ages*. London: Macdonald, 1951.

Richardson, Alan, and Geoff Hughes. *Ancient Magicks for a New Age*. St. Paul, MN: Llewellyn Publications, 1992.

Rogers, Guy MacLean. *The Mysteries of Artemis of Ephesos: Cult, Polis, and Change in the Graeco-Roman World*. New Haven, CT: Yale University Press, 2012.

Sallust. *On the Gods and the World*. Translated by Thomas Taylor. Los Angeles, CA: Philosophical Research Society, 1976.

Scholem, Gershom. *The Origins of the Kabbalah*. Princeton: Princeton University Press, 1990.

Schramm, Ken. *The Compleat Meadmaker: Home Production of Honey Wine From Your First Batch to Award-Winning Fruit and Herb Variations*. Boulder, CO: Brewers Publications, 2003.

Stevenson, David. *The Origins of Freemasonry: Scotland's Century, 1590–1710*. Cambridge: Cambridge University Press, 1988.

Stewart, R. J., ed. *The Book of Merlin: Insights from the Merlin Conference*. London: Blandford Press, 1987.

———, ed. *Merlin and Woman: The Book of the Second Merlin Conference*. London: Blandford Press, 1988.

———. *The Mystic Life of Merlin*. London: Routledge & Kegan Paul, 1986.

———. *The Prophetic Vision of Merlin*. London: Routledge & Kegan Paul, 1986.

———. "The Tomb of a King," in *The UnderWorld Initiation: A Journey Towards Psychic Transformation*. Wellingborough, UK: Aquarian, 1985.

———. *The Way of Merlin*. London: HarperCollins, 1991.

Sullivan, William. *The Secret of the Incas: Myth, Astronomy, and the War Against Time*. New York: Crown, 1997.

Tolkien, J. R. R. *Beowulf: A Translation and Commentary*. Boston: Houghton Mifflin Harcourt, 2014.

Tolstoy, Nikolai. *The Quest for Merlin*. Boston: Little, Brown, 1985.

Weston, Jessie. *From Ritual to Romance*. Gloucester, MA: Peter Smith, 1983.

Williams ab Ithel, J., ed. *The Barddas of Iolo Morganwg*. York Beach, ME: Weiser, 2004.

Index

To Write to the Author

If you wish to contact the author or would like more information about this book, please write to the author in care of Llewellyn Worldwide Ltd. and we will forward your request. Both the author and publisher appreciate hearing from you and learning of your enjoyment of this book and how it has helped you. Llewellyn Worldwide Ltd. cannot guarantee that every letter written to the author can be answered, but all will be forwarded. Please write to:

John Michael Greer
℅ Llewellyn Worldwide
2143 Wooddale Drive
Woodbury, MN 55125-2989

Please enclose a self-addressed stamped envelope for reply,
or $1.00 to cover costs. If outside the U.S.A., enclose
an international postal reply coupon.

Many of Llewellyn's authors have websites with additional information and resources. For more information, please visit our website at http://www.llewellyn.com.